Beulah C Garretson

Fireside Fancies

Beulah C Garretson

Fireside Fancies

ISBN/EAN: 9783337254209

Printed in Europe, USA, Canada, Australia, Japan

Cover: Foto ©Andreas Hilbeck / pixelio.de

More available books at **www.hansebooks.com**

FIRESIDE FANCIES

BY

BEULAH C. GARRETSON

PHILADELPHIA & LONDON
J. B. LIPPINCOTT COMPANY
1899

PS 1734
.G145 F5

TO THE MEMORY

OF

MY FATHER

AND TO

MY MOTHER

I DEDICATE THIS LITTLE
VOLUME

Contents

Contents

Fireside Fancies

THE world outside is white and silent. The bare branches of the trees stretch themselves a black and ghostly tracery against the gleaming background. The dark pines throw strange fantastic shadows quite in harmony with the low weird music caused by the gentle breath of wind as it sweeps lightly over them. Above all the solemn, star-strewn vault of heaven. Intensely blue and cold and far away it looks with its myriads of other worlds unconcernedly holding their allotted place in the universe.

On such a night the warm glow of the blazing logs offers an inducement not to be resisted; one willingly succumbs to the cheery influence of the fitful firelight and idly falls to watching the smoke as it curls lazily upward and out through the dark

7

throat of the chimney. No light save of the ruddy flames as they flicker and dance in capricious play now here, now there, blazing gayly one minute, the next sinking down to a faint blue light.

It is very attractive, very seductive to thought ; one quickly falls to dreaming,— dreaming about everything, about nothing, phantom chases phantom through the brain, the mind but half conscious of the kaleidoscopic movement as each figure gives place to the next, some grave, some gay, some bringing a tender smile, others a half-suppressed sigh.

There is no sound but that of the crackling logs, the world with its busy rush and turmoil is shut out, forgotten for the time, and silence reigns. That profound stillness which is so helpful, so restful, where no jarring sound disturbs the half-formed thought or mocks the dreamer's earnest mood. From this silence may be claimed a truer knowledge of life and of self. At such a time one may meet and greet his own identity, analyze each thought and action in a curious, impersonal manner, rather as one would examine minutely some specimen of the genus homo placed under a glass case in a museum and his individuality laid bare for inspection.

An English writer has said there is much help in silence. From its touch we gain renewed life. Silence is to the soul what his mother earth is to Briareus, from contact with it we rise healed of our hurts and strengthened for the fight.

"Amid the babel of the schools we stand bewildered and affrighted. Silence gives us peace and hope. Silence teaches us no creed, only that God's arms are around the universe.

"How small and unimportant seem our fretful troubles and ambitions when we stand with them in our hand before the great, calm face of silence! We smile at them and are ashamed.

"Silence teaches us how little we are,—how great we are. In the world's market-places we are tinkers, tailors, apothecaries, thieves,—respectable or otherwise, as the case may be,—mere atoms of a mighty machine,—mere insects in a vast hive. It is only in silence that it comes home to us that we are something much greater than this,—that we are men,—with all the universe and with all eternity before us."

With this solemn stillness come more earnest thoughts ; the mind wanders back over the years already gone, pausing to gaze in contemplation at the mile-stones that mark the way passed over. With what eager hope and joyful aspirations were some approached ! with hopes that blessed in their fruition or turned to dust and ashes in the mouth, while some were passed with aching heart and eyes averted.

In the spring-time of life these mile-stones hold all the mystical attraction the future contains. With head erect and firm, unfaltering feet, we go forth to meet and pass them. Fearlessly, curiously indeed, do we hurry forward, chiding impatiently the slower gait of our elders, with whom for courtesy's sake we must try to keep apace to lend to their lagging steps a supporting arm, for, the zenith of life reached, they are in no such haste to cover the distance between one mile-stone and the next.

Fireside Fancies

Hot and dusty the road stretches out before them, while cool and restful is the shade of yonder tree.

But in the fulness of time the journey must be taken, it is inevitable ; on and still on we go, penetrating the future, living, enjoying, regretting, only to repeat the same again and again, for our lives change almost imperceptibly, scene follows scene with such quiet persistency that we scarcely realize when one begins or when it fades away. Always we are looking forward, planning, hoping, aspiring.

In this flickering, uncertain firelight one's thoughts naturally fall upon the vicissitudes of human life, —how like it is to the flame before us ! At first only a feeble spark which has to be coaxed along, then a flame more or less brilliant, a gradual loss of light and heat, and then a bed of embers which slowly die one by one. If that were all, truly the game would not be worth the candle. But to return once more to the simile. When the first faint spark appears and is breaking into a glow, with what care and interest is it watched, how, when the feeble life seems about to go out, do we tend and help it, and what gratified pleasure do we experience when it breaks into a cheerful blaze and gives to us the warmth and comfort to which our care is entitled !

With keenest pleasure do we watch its ever-varying moods, a little anxious when it mounts too high, satisfied and at ease when it burns with steady, quiet purpose. Safest that for any life.

Then comes the gradual loss of power. But what matters that ! While it lived it served its purpose. Light, warmth, heat, pleasure it gave, to all who sought it,—gave freely and without stint of all that it had to give. Its life was beautiful and useful. The dying embers glowing with the same steady purpose to the end, the light softer, more tender, until the last faint gleam had gone. Well done can be its record too. And for it also the law of correlation brings a resurrection, for the dead ashes are cast forth upon the barren earth and in the spring a new life rises from them.

In the waning light one falls to wondering how he would have shaped his course could he have foreseen the future, wondering if he has used his talents to the best advantage, if he has made a man of himself worthy of some younger life following in his footsteps. There are many to watch and be influenced by his manner of living.

The thought is disturbing to the waking dreamer, and he is glad to have his ideas diverted by a sudden shower of sparks followed by a cheerful blaze.

But again he falls to probing the obscurity of the future, trying to fathom what it holds in store for him, and wondering how he is prepared to meet and face the unknown.

This great mysterious future which holds such a fascination for all! Much better we should not know what lies before us, what dark hours must fall to our lot, for in that case the knowledge would prove such a grievous burden as to quite unfit us for bearing ourselves bravely when the time of trouble arrives. No matter how dark the present, for the future there is always hope.

Life means so much to some, so little to

others. It is true circumstances do shape our destinies, but often it is possible to so shape those circumstances as to bring about a much better result. We are too apt to let matters drift and so shape themselves.

To succeed in any attempt means constant care—eternal vigilance.

It is a great fashion people have of waiting, Macawber-like, for something to turn up. Give me an opportunity, set me some great task, then I will show the world what I can do. This is their cry, oblivious, apparently, to the fact that most people have to carve out their own fortunes. It is only by faithfully and conscientiously performing such duties as come to them in relation to the minor affairs of life that they are prepared to cope with the really great problem when it is presented. These small every-day matters seem very trivial and unimportant, yet are of vast account in order to keep the tenor of life well balanced. Training is one of the vital points of living.

It is comparatively easy to attempt the

mastery of things great, the successful ac-
complishment of which brings praise and
honor.   But it is the things small, the
wee little pin-pricks of life, that show of
what stuff one is really made.   It requires
true heroism to live above these apparently
trifling matters which occur every hour of
the day—every day of the year.   To accomplish this with serene face and unruffled
brow means victory, indeed, but it brings no
laurels with it.   This silent, unseen victory
over self is worthy of the highest praise, all
the more because it has been helped on by
no word of cheer or encouragement.   It
is a wonderful help to hear a word of praise
occasionally, an acknowledgment that the
effort made is appreciated.

Life is a mystery for most, meaning much
more to some than to others ; with the inevitable end, death, for all.   How fearfully
some advance to meet it, how fearlessly
others !   Yet why should any one fear ?
true, no one knows what lies beyond, but
why fear because of that?

If it is the parting of the ego from the
body, why should not that same fear be

experienced each night? Yet how gladly
we lay our tired bodies down upon the
bed to rest, quite conscious that in a short
time, through the agency of that mystic
power, sleep, the ego will have parted company with the body as effectually as though
they had never been a part of each other.

No one denies that sleep is other than
a great blessing, yet who looks upon
death as anything but a misfortune when
it comes in the vigor of life.

While we sleep the something left lying
upon the bed is nothing but an inert mass
of bones and tissue, the individuality may
be thousands of miles away utterly unconscious of the now useless body.

As one never considers the daytime
body as in any way unusual, so it is with
the dream body : whatever it may be, it is
quite as useful for the purpose and quite
as much a matter of course as the more
substantial one of flesh and blood.

To compare sleep and death would seem
to do away with all fear regarding the
hereafter.

Death is but a prolonged sleep for the

body,—the ego, that something which makes man other than a soulless image, is free as air; clothed in whatever form it may be, again it is all-sufficient for the purpose. There can be no regret for the old body laid aside any more than in our dreams our daytime bodies are missed. With new surroundings they have ceased to be necessary.

Looked upon in this light death remains a mystery, but holds no terror.

As we live it may be our hereafter is influenced,—who can say? As the man's intelligence is greater than the child's, so perhaps wisdom and knowledge will increase with changed environments.

At all events, it is certainly worse than useless to worry about what we do not and cannot know. What all do know is, that as we live wisely and in accordance with nature's laws so much more satisfaction and happiness do we gain from our present existence, and whatever may lie before us in the life beyond the grave good deeds and manly actions are not likely to jeopardize the future.

COBWEBS

DELICATE cobwebs of fancy are the thoughts that festoon themselves from corner to corner of the brain. Vague, uncertain, and shadowy as the gossamer fabric that gives them a name. Marvellous and complicated are they during their mystic progress through the brain.

Never is this mass of gray matter inactive. Even while the body is at rest the mind continues to work.

How subtle are some of these fancies! too elusive are they to even make an effort to grasp them. Such are the dew-drops on the web, which the sunlight of consecutive thought causes to disappear even while it is in the act of stretching out a detaining hand.

Like some gorgeous-winged creature, these fantastic fancies pause for an instant in their aerial flight, only to vanish before one becomes fully conscious of their presence.

Cobwebs

Dainty and airy and dim are these fragile fancies of light. The filmy cords reached out to stay and chain them prove how ineffectual they are for so difficult a task.

At first mere threads, reaching out they make fast one end, then another and another, until a foundation is formed on which to work out the intricate pattern. Little by little it grows and grows, gaining strength and shape with each additional effort.

The busy insect worker has his purpose too ; laboriously he works to sustain life. He too, must have method, ways and means. He weaves his web that he may live. It seems a cruel purpose, yet all things prey upon some other. Here also it is still the survival of the fittest. How energetic and tireless is this hurrying little creature racing back and forth with incredible speed ! too rapid is his work to seem to admit of any design ; yet how symmetrical, how perfect is the finished product ! how exquisite is it when spread upon grass or hedgerow, glistening and sparkling with cups of crystal and jewels left by the elf-folk in their hurry to escape to the mossy greenwood before the first faint gleams of crimson and gold appear to streak the eastern sky and bid a glad good-morning to the refreshed earth, proclaiming by their presence the advent of another day !

More substantial than these vanishing fairy fabrics are the cobwebs of thought woven by the human worker.

From small beginnings can great things come ; so small and insignificant at first as scarce to attract one instant's notice ; yet the filmy thread of thought has come in some way, and there it clings firmly fastened to the brain, swaying about in sympathy with those other thoughts, whose right to remain securely anchored have been proved by their worth. Side by side with them is this other thought, although scarce worthy of so meaning a name ; more of a vague suggestion is it, until at last another thread reaches out in search of some support, and finding this loose, swaying end, clings fast to it and forms a perfect connection, the two fulfilling their destiny and proving their right to recognition, their special use, and their own particular place in fitting in with the general scheme.

Nearly all thoughts are filmy embryos at first, rarely do they spring from the brain full grown, like Minerva from the head of Jupiter, but are the consequence of a series of ideas, one evolved from another, gaining meaning as they approach maturity.

❧❧❧

THE TIME IS NOW

IN reply to the inquiries of his friends as to why he did not give to the world the results of his earnest thoughts and studies, Joubert's answer was, " It is not yet time." And again, after the years had passed and still his pen remained inactive, his reply to the same question was, "The time has passed." So it is with many lives, they mean to do, the desire is there,—a desire which is at some time in some vague way to be fulfilled ; but they live on and on, and still they feel it is not yet time, until all at once they are shocked by the realization that the time is past,—it is too late.

One reason for letting the hours slip by so unprofitably is the fear of failing in an undertaking, the feeling that rather than make only a partial success it were better to let the opportunity go entirely. But surely it is better to fail from excess of courage than from lack of it. All beginnings must necessarily be imperfect, that is inevitable, so why let the fact discourage one from further effort? It should be an incentive to try again and yet again, profiting by each mistake until at last something is accomplished worthy of recognition. Each step makes the next one easier and the goal just that much nearer. No one should permit the thought to take root that it is not yet time, for it is always the right time to make use of the one or the ten talents possessed. Unless used and so multiplied they are worse than wasted. It is a positive crime to possess and yet ignore and trample underfoot the ability that might be so productive of good.

The Time is Now

Thank God for the one talent, however small; cultivate it and make much of it, for so only will it increase, bringing a rich compensation.

It is childish to cry aloud in anger and despair, because only one talent has been given it is useless to try and make anything of it. It is such as these who prove themselves unworthy of even the smallest gift; they let the days go, and as each one passes their faculties become rusty from disuse and incapable of effort. Presently the time comes when sorely against their wills they are forced to say with Joubert it is too late, the time has passed.

There is a whole world of pathos in those few words. They tell of a life that has meant well, but of indecision and doubt; of a desire to begin some real work, of a longing for some tangible object in life, of the many beginnings which have all fallen short of fulfilment. They tell of the talent hidden in the napkin and buried.

The destiny of the human race is without doubt the perfect man. But how attain such lofty heights? There is but

one way.   By using and using wisely the
faculties born of intelligence.   By being
satisfied with small beginnings, for so only
can great ends be attained.   To advance,
to climb upward in safety must be by
each step of the ladder, round by round.
But man is ambitious.   The top of the
ladder does not seem very high, a short
run and a quick jump should effect a foot-
ing ; it takes too long and is too monotonous to climb up one step at a time.   But
it is only the patient climbers who remain
at the top when it is once reached.   Occasionally the impatient ones do reach the
top, but how long do they remain there?
Dazzled by the success of their experiment,
they ignore all the laws which are meant
for ordinary mortals, look upon themselves
as demigods, and act accordingly.   The
fall that follows is, indeed, crushing and
terrible.   Witness, for example, Napoleon.
Did those few brilliant years of camp and
court life compensate him for the weary
hours of mental and physical suffering he
passed on his island prison ?

Slowly and surely doing whatever comes

next is a safeguard for all lives. So only can they get the training which makes them capable of action and worthy to sustain power when the time comes. Proficiency in little things make great achievements possible.

But to be always putting things off. To be saying with Talleyrand never do to-day what can be put off till to-morrow is to dwarf the mentally and put a clog on the wheels of time. Talleyrand was disappointed and embittered, and showed the littleness of his nature by warping and distorting his naturally great abilities. His moral sense was out of tune.

It is not always easy to do with undisturbed serenity that which comes next, to try and weave a smooth web from a tangled thread. But the skein of life is full of knots that only the utmost patience can untie. Too much luxury and ease enfeeble the mind as well as the body. To be strong and vigorous there must be exercise for both brain and muscle. The body cannot be strong unless nerves and tissues are in good condition, neither can the mind be in a fit state to cope with problems unless it has accustomed itself from constant practice to weigh and consider carefully each action, each question, not only as it relates to itself but to the world at large, for the radiation of a thought is like that made by a pebble falling in the water. No one can suffer alone. Our lives are so closely blended with those of others that what affects one must in a measure affect all. The egoist becomes a stumbling-block in the path of many. In reading the biographies of those who have become famous one is made to realize his own littleness ; to appreciate the fact that his sufferings are but the common lot of all. In the quick poignancy of our misery we are apt to think that we alone have burdens too heavy to be borne, while others are gay, happy, and successful. We are, the most of us, so wrapt up in our own personality that we do not give half recognition to that of others.

Because others have been successful we allow ourselves to be discouraged, and to think the gayety and happiness is all for

them, with no prospect of any for ourselves.

But underneath and back of the gayety
and happiness in what the world calls success there too often lurks the sting of un-
fulfilled desire, a grief at being unable to
accomplish that which is nearest the heart.

Of the men and women of whom we are
one we see but the outside, their surface
selves, the accomplished result. That which
cannot be seen, and is only dimly guessed
at, is the inner life with its many struggles.
Of the failure after failure, of the bitterness of defeat which well-nigh causes them
to give up the battle, we know nothing.
But the really earnest worker will not ac-
knowledge defeat. From his very failures
he reaps the experience that at last brings
success, that success which the world sees
and applauds and thinks in its ignorance is
easily won.

Many are the silent tragedies enacted
in the helpless almost hopeless battling
with self and circumstances. But this is
the side of success the world knows nothing of.

Fireside Fancies

When defeat and despair are forever staring us out of countenance it is hard indeed to foster the least spark of courage. But

> " Lives of great men all remind us
> We can make our lives sublime,
> And departing leave behind us
> Footprints on the sands of time. "

When we read of their brave struggles with hardships, of the poverty and disease which many of them had to encounter, it gives us the courage to emulate their example, to try if we too cannot leave footprints on the sands of time. They surmounted difficulty after difficulty, and by sheer determination and force of character were able to rise above circumstances and make for themselves name and place in the annals of history. By their own misfortunes they were able to appreciate the needs of others and to do their share in the world's work in the sphere opened to them. They became what they were because they preferred to be themselves at whatever cost rather than a more or less good imitation of some one else.

28

Stability of Character

Each one is but a unit in this mighty universe. Much of the trouble in life comes from a failure to realize this fact, but to think instead his own particular self is or ought to be the axis around which his own particular world should revolve.

There is but one axis, and God that one. We are the spokes in the wheel of time. While we fill our place with patience and unswerving fidelity all is well. But if we are weak and faltering the whole structure is affected by our indecision and want of stability. Chaos must result.

And so the time to think and act is always now, this very hour, this very minute; to-morrow it may be too late.

❦❦❦

STABILITY OF CHARACTER

THE old saying, a rolling stone gathers no moss, although trite, is true enough to bear endless repetition.

Think well, choose carefully, then stick, is the secret of success. To do that requires that stability of character which might surely be ranked among the cardinal virtues. Without it one rarely acquires a secure position. Vacillation portrays a weakness that is apt to bring ruin, both moral and financial, in its train.

The man who tries one thing after another, leaving each because all is not just according to his fancy, soon becomes a rolling stone. As the years pass he will find it harder and harder to adapt himself to circumstances and, what will prove more trying still, to a subordinate position, for that is all he can expect or command until he has made himself competent to fill one of trust.

There are comparatively few utterly devoid of ambition and of ability more or less marked in some direction. To be successful it is necessary to begin the cultivation of that ability at the very start and to continue it whenever and wherever opportunity offers. For seldom is greatness thrust upon one, and when it is, it is a short-lived glory not always desirable. To be great requires industry, and above all perseverance. Without stability of character the one is as impossible as the other.

There is a class of uncertain individuals who never know their own minds for five minutes consecutively ; to be obliged to be with them is absolutely maddening, one never knows what to expect, for they are merely an echo of the last speaker. There is such a comfortable feeling of security in turning to one whose opinions and advice are worth something, because never given without first being carefully considered. The first step toward success lies in the formation of a firm, independent individuality ; unless the firmness degenerates into what is commonly known as pig-headedness, the holder will find many prizes awaiting him on his journey through life, and life itself will mean more to him, his outlook will be broader, freer, hemmed in by none of the petty fears that beset the path of a weaker character.

A steady perseverance in the line of work chosen is sure to bring some measure of success. It is the only possible way to attain it. That goal is reached only by going straight ahead, turning neither to the right nor to the left. No man's life is long enough to traverse three or four different ways, even although a fair promise of success, luring him on, may lie at the end of each. One only can be gone over, and by hesitating too long which one to select the traveller will be apt to find himself in the same predicament as was "B'rer Fox" in regard to the barbecues.

The world is so full of beautiful and interesting things that there is absolutely no excuse for any one living an entirely aimless existence. Among so much, something surely could be found that would prove of paramount interest to each individual, the pursuit of which would add zest to life. Few minds are wholly vacuous. Not many feel that living means only a passing of time, days to be gotten through some way. For most "life is real, life is earnest;" considered in that way it has many good things to offer. But for the lazy idler it means little, because of the fact that he is a lazy idler. While he remains such it will never mean anything more. But let him realize he is a man, firm in strength to meet and overcome obstacles rather than be overcome by them, and matters will soon assume a different aspect. He will then feel himself a man among men, which is much more conducive to self-respect than to be forced to feel one's self a pigmy among giants.

Firmness is one thing, obstinacy quite another; it is right and just to hold to one's own opinions, but the mistake is so often made in thinking that because they are one's own they must necessarily be correct. First be very sure they are right, then stick to them, allowing others a like privilege.

It is a very easy matter to fall into any habit, and the possessors of strong, decided wills are apt to become arbitrary. What they think and say must be accepted as final. They allow no discussion concerning it. It is probably an unconscious habit at first, but it grows with startling rapidity and soon becomes a grievous fault. Every one should have the right to give expression to his own ideas, whether right or wrong ; if a reasonable being, he is open to conviction ; if not, if he be one of those men who holds to his own opinions though the skies fall, argument is of no avail, they are not of sufficient importance for any one to take the time to attempt to combat them. But for all the fine disregard we would like to show they are absolutely exasperating, these people ! We are too human yet not to feel the sting of being calmly set aside and ignored.

To always agree would be dreadfully monotonous. A good-natured argument is both instructive and interesting ; the point of view seldom being the same in any two cases, a comparison of ideas follows from which much may be gained. The method of instruction used by the early sages partook more of the form of argument than of a discourse. To be effective an argument must be just and carried on without loss of temper. The most brilliant speaker becomes weak when once he loses his self-control. Cicero was the most wonderful orator of his time so long as he said what he liked without interruption or interference, but the moment any one presumed to differ with him he lost his greatness because he lost his temper. No one can be truly great who does not respect the rights of others. To be master of one's self is to be master of the world, because it means the ability backed by the desire to overcome difficulties.

A man is seldom so unfortunate as to be hampered all his life with unsurmountable obstacles. If he has it in him he must and will rise to whatever heights he is capable of holding. In the beginning all doors are open to him, what he becomes he makes himself. Emerson has said, "Nature arms each man with some faculty which enables him to do easily some feat impossible to any other, and thus makes him necessary to society." Not many realize how true this is ; because this something seems small and insignificant it may be thrust aside as not worth the doing, whereas it is the little things that have so much to do with the comfort of one's surroundings ; these seeming nothings smooth and polish off the rough surfaces and jagged corners. If more attention were paid to rounding off these corners and less to making them prominent, many hurts would be avoided. But nearly every one wants to lead, and as a consequence many are injured in the mad race to get ahead. It is just as impossible for every one to be first as for all to be last. The line lengthens out indefinitely with a place for all, giving plenty of room for free movement. In all times and in all places it has been the survival of the fittest. Whatsoever place a man is capable of filling, it is there waiting for him to step into without the necessity of any being pushed aside. There is room for all in the front ranks, which are not so well filled as are some others.

ADAPTABILITY

To adapt one's self to circumstances gracefully is a most desirable faculty to possess, but it must be confessed it is rather

Adaptability

a rare gift. To accept the position in which
one is placed, making the best of it and
the most of it, is a much easier way out of
a difficulty than to sink down in despair
with a thoroughly discouraged can't help
air. It may be bad, very bad, indeed, but,
as a rule, it might be worse. To consider
it in this light does much to remove bar-
riers and bring about a better condition of
things. But troubles and annoyances have
a way of magnifying if they meet with the
least bit of encouragement that soon heap
up mountains in the paths of all who do
not set to work earnestly to overcome
them.

God meant every one to be happy and
healthful both in mind and body. When
troubles come through our own indiscre-
tions or from other causes, He did not
mean that we should entirely succumb to
them and let them darken our lives for all
time. But to all human beings He has
given reason and intelligence to enable
them to cope with the difficulties and
problems by which they have surrounded
themselves.

Fireside Fancies

God gave to us all intelligence,
And meant us to use it aright,
To ennoble the world we live in,
To bring out of the darkness—light.

He fashioned men in his own likeness,
Meaning them to be Godlike too.
Not selfish and sordid and wicked,
But honest and noble and true.

And so, having been endowed with the divine faculty of intellect, we are in duty bound to exert it for our own benefit as well as for others.

If things always went right and one had everything one wanted, life would very soon become monotonous. A desire gratified as soon as expressed gives, as a rule, very little pleasure. We are so constituted that in order to properly value a thing the possession of it must be hedged around with difficulties.

People surrounded by every luxury, living the lives of petted exotics, are not the fortunate individuals they are popularly supposed to be ; quite the reverse, indeed, for they are not fulfilling their destinies or using their God-given faculties. They are rusting out and losing half the zest of living. Many people have never been guilty of one useful action in all their lives. Not that they are incompetent or unwilling, only nothing has ever been demanded or expected of them, and so it does not occur to them that it might be desirable to take some active part in this work-a-day world. Sometimes these apparently useless creatures are made to realize what an objectless existence they are leading, and in consequence astonish their friends with their ability to do for themselves and others. Before, their faculties were lying dormant and becoming clogged from disuse.

In this busy world of ups and downs one must be up and doing if he wishes to swim with the tide, for the drones go down and are soon swept under ; even the eddy they make in sinking is but for a moment.

Too much luxury is enervating and produces a sybarite. A moderate amount is, on the contrary, helpful and refining. It must be easier to have beautiful thoughts and encourage high aspirations amid attractive surroundings than where all is wretchedness and poverty, although it must be acknowledged some of the grandest philosophy of living has come to us from the bare cells of self-imposed poverty.

But the nineteenth century has outgrown self-inflicted trials. The philosopher of to-day can live a much fuller and rounder existence by living the life of a gentleman and a man of the world, where his influence and ideas can extend to the many instead of being confined to a favored few. An honorable man who leads a consistent life does far greater good in this day than did ever Diogenes in his tub, the walls of which were too confined to allow the rays of his lantern to penetrate far enough into the gloom for him to find that honest man for whom he was so long searching. Had he oftener stepped out from his narrow quarters and given to his world the example of an honest man, he might sooner have found another.

INDIVIDUAL INFLUENCE

IT is a wonderful thing to think of and should give one a feeling of heavy responsibility to know that as we individually live we help to make the world what it is.

As we mould our characters so are our immediate surroundings colored, and that coloring extends much farther afield than we have any idea; and as a matter of course the stronger and more pronounced the characteristics the farther is the influence felt. Could we but keep in mind these few words so fraught with meaning for ourselves and others : " Nor knowest thou what argument thy life to thy neighbor's creed has lent !" Only a few words, but like many another sentence from Emerson's pen they convey a meaning to live by.

No one is so insignificant but some atmosphere surrounds him.

Can it be expected that our children will be capable of exerting a wise and just influence upon the world when their time comes unless we set them the example? For many years they are mere parrots, copying the ways of their elders. By the time they have arrived at an age to think for themselves their habits are formed, and they seldom change them to any great extent. The foundation once laid, the shape and style of the subsequent structure must retain virtually the same form to the end. Laying the foundation of a human life is the most important epoch in its career.

It is we who are the makers of the history of to-day. Yet it is to be feared many would be sorry to read the record, if, indeed, they recognized it as of their own making. For, after all, a great part of the failings of humanity are due to thoughtlessness ; a hasty word or an unwise act may be followed by the most dire results, the consequences of which may be the undoing of more than one life.

It is not expected that any one should

be perfect, but every one has a right to expect thoughtfulness and consideration on the part of others. That is an imperative duty each individual owes to the world at large, for the influence that is a part of every human being is something very real and an unconscious element in the lives of all with whom they are thrown. Qualities to be admired and emulated or guarded against are met with almost hourly.

The world is such a rushing, driving, busy place that few seem to have time, or perhaps will not take it, to make individuals of themselves, but would seem to be satisfied with being one of the people, thinking little as to which way the tide is carrying them. Or it may be that the majority are so interested in their own personality that they do not quite try to understand that of others ; this unconscious egotism making them the all-important subject. Because their affairs are of vital moment to themselves they, without exactly meaning to do so, demand a like interest from others. What we think and what we do affects not only ourselves, but every one with whom we come in touch. The individuality of a person is evident without verbal utterance.

It is a privilege, indeed, to meet a person whose good breeding is shown in every word and glance, whose effort is not to dazzle by his own superior attainments but to encourage and draw out the best in his companion ; they inspire one with confidence in one's own abilities and suggest thoughts worth something. Having some definite aim in life, their individuality is decided. Such people are like a tonic, rousing all the sleeping energy of one's nature, and for a time at least make one long to be up and doing,—yes, and something worth the doing, too.

True refinement makes itself felt amid any surroundings, and is accorded due recognition. Such a one does not need to herald his accomplishments, whatever they may be ; they are evident only at such times when it is desirable they should be. Loud and boisterous behavior stamps the actor as innately vulgar, no matter in what sphere of life he may belong. The continual placing of one's self *en evidence* is essentially ill-bred, and must denote a shallow nature.

The influence that makes itself felt rather than heard is the more effective of the two. The unspoken word, the look or action so filled with meaning, will carry greater weight than the most long-winded argument on the error of one's ways, for that only serves to antagonize and to confirm one in his own views more strongly than ever. The spirit of contradiction latent in every nature is immediately brought to the surface. The more didactic the discourse becomes the greater grows the belief as to the opponent's mistaken judgment. Little or no good, results ; the reverse is more apt to be the case.

There are people whose attitude toward mankind in general is one of defence ; with such it is well-nigh impossible to avoid conflict ; they unconsciously approach every one from that stand-point, and as one quickly feels the influence of another personality he at once becomes self-assertive, and to be on the defensive is necessarily to be at a disadvantage. Argumentative people are to be dreaded for more reasons than one. They do an immense amount of harm. If one is always on the lookout for the seamy side in human nature he is pretty apt to find it. It is expecting the worst that has much to do with the downward career of man. One false step, and the community is ever ready to give him an onward push. Perhaps a helping hand held out to offer a moral support would save much future crime. There need be no fear of contamination ; it is only the weak who are easily swayed. But with every man's hand against them it is little wonder these unfortunates so soon become desperate outcasts, showing no mercy, having no pity. From their stand-point why should they? Was any mercy shown them? It is man's inhumanity to man that has made them what they are.

TRUE TO ONE'S SELF

"BE true to thyself." Years ago our tender poet, Longfellow, wrote these words to his German friend Freiligrath. It is a watchword that might well be engraven on the heart of every man and woman. Ay, be true to thyself, and let thy watch-fire burn clear and bright, lighting thee and many another by its pure glow to a safe haven at last.

True to one's self! it seems a simple thing, yet of how many can it be truthfully said that they are true to themselves, true to their convictions at all costs! It is never pleasant to be in the minority, and requires real moral courage to espouse the unpopular side even when convinced of its righteousness. It is far easier to say nothing than to oppose the multitude.

But how would evils ever be righted unless some one was found to champion the cause and stand firm in his belief and to set the ball rolling? Like the one of snow,

47

it gathers volume as it rolls, and finally attains proportions vast enough to annihilate opposing forces. It cannot be denied that reformers frequently become fanatics, but the ultimate result of their fanaticism is good. All reforms must be evolved from extremes. History gives many terrible examples of what it meant in early times to be true to one's self. But, thank God! such dastardly crimes are no more, but are gone with the only too recent years when man took a grim pleasure in seeing his fellow-man stretched upon the rack or torn limb from limb because, forsooth, opinions differed. Now man may be true to himself without incurring any more serious consequences than the disapprobation or possible censure of others,—surely nothing very terrible in itself, and easily borne if one feels assured he is in the right.

One of the existing evils of this age, perhaps of all ages, has been lack of purpose. A few there are with a definite goal. Their whole lives, every action, centres at one point. But the majority do as others do, drift as the stream carries them. It is much easier and pleasanter, and requires very little mental exertion.

Many a long day will have passed away, many a nation be gathered to its fathers, before the world is composed of individuals with sufficient moral courage and mental stamina to stand alone, when each one shall be the product of his own individuality, to whom these lines can no longer be applied with any degree of truth :

" And we have been on many thousand lines,
 And we have shown on each talent and power,
 But hardly have we, for one little hour,
 Been on our own line, have we been ourselves ;
 Hardly had skill to utter one of all
 The nameless feelings that course through our breast,
 But they course on forever unexpressed.
 And long we try in vain to speak and act
 Our hidden self, and what we say and do
 Is eloquent, is well—but 'tis not true."

And again the same poet says,—

" I knew the mass of men concealed
 Their thoughts, for fear that if revealed
 They would by other men be met

Fireside Fancies

With blank indifference or with blame reproved ;
I knew they lived and moved
Tricked in disguises alien to the rest
Of men and alien to themselves—and yet
The same heart beats in every human breast."

Alas ! that it should be so that the real
and the true is constantly being withheld
because of the fear of being misunderstood, and that very fear is often the cause
of bringing about just what we have been
trying to avoid. Often we are thought
heartless and indifferent because we have
been unwilling or unable to express our
real feelings, and the true sympathy that
animates our hearts. From timidity or
indifference we permit others to form a
very unjust estimate of our characters.

To be true to one's self and one's convictions includes the rather paradoxical
meaning of giving up and accepting—
tacitly, at least—the opinions of some one
else, for to stick doggedly to one idea,
ignoring the same right to others, is only
to harm the cause, whereas sometimes a
partial acceptance of another's theories
brings about a most amicable understand-

ing in the end, and in many cases the premise will be found to have been the same, only so differently clothed that recognition at first sight was impossible.

Why stick stubbornly to one course when it makes absolutely no difference in the universe whether it shall be one way or another, or indeed, very often, whether it shall be at all? Such a character is simply an epitome of obstinacy and consummate selfishness. That is not being true to one's self, but is merely a determination to have one's own way at all costs.

To be mentally true, morally true, is humanizing and refining to a greater extent than any other one thing. It is one of the most important elements in the progress of the world and in the evolution of society. It does away with apathy and promotes vitality; in a word, it creates the thinking man out of the animal man.

Truth, they say, is found at the bottom of a well. Why not on the surface? People are too busy to stop and dredge for a commodity that should be the hourly need of every community. But while man continues to exercise all his ingenuity in trying to outwit his neighbor it goes without saying that the neighbor needs watching. If there was a little less scheming and a little more honesty the result would be an immense gain in every department of home, state, and nation, the saving of monetary expense to city and government would soon amount to enough to pay off the national debt, while the saving of moral and mental expense would prove a far more valuable boon to mankind. But while every man is obliged to suspect his brother, he has very little time left to cultivate a better side to his nature. To live in accord with the golden rule does sound extremely Utopian, but it certainly would save a great deal of trouble.

FRIENDSHIP

The term friend is one of the most frequently misapplied words in use. While one is often attracted toward others, enjoys their society, may even like to see them daily, one does not in the least feel for them that deeper sensation caused by the sacred tie that binds two lives together in real friendship. That is something quite different from the feeling experienced for the host of people generally designated by that title,—people whose companionship is a pleasure, for they are bright, charming, witty, and interesting, much more attractive to all outward appearances than the few whom we have taken into our hearts and for whom we feel a real friendship. Just why it is we love them it is hard to say ; it is not for any particular qualities easy to name. They may not have any of the attributes that would seem to fit into and form a complement to our own nature. All we know or can say is, that we do love them. They give to us a something impossible to describe, but satisfying and restful to receive.

Between friends of this kind is that perfect understanding that renders words unnecessary in times of intense feeling, of deep emotion. There is an unspoken sympathy and understanding of the other's mood.

Such a friendship is indeed rare, but the possession is priceless. A friend is as jealous of our honor as we ourselves. With him conversation is more natural than with others because of the assurance of being understood, and the fear of a wrong construction being put upon a thoughtless word or action is entirely done away with ; no repetition of our words by a friend will place us in a false light with others.

They say marriages are made in heaven ; if that is so then friendships must be formed just outside the gates.

History gives many instances of this tie between man and man, woman and woman, and man and woman. In the life of the ordinary mortal, hemmed around by conventionalities, the latter is so rare as to be almost unique, yet of them all is the most satisfying ; because of the contrast between the two natures they have more to give each other.

It is difficult to keep a friendship of this kind, because there is always some one to place a wrong construction upon it, to indulge in covert sneers and innuendoes, to affirm the impossibility of such a thing existing, and for them it could not exist. The very fact of their doubting the purity of the motive proves that for them it would be impossible. They naturally judge from their own stand-point. As a matter of course, such unkind criticism does much toward marring the pleasure of the intercourse, and is almost sure in time to bring about a rupture, thus robbing two lives of much innocent happiness and mutual aid. If let alone they would have rounded out each other's existence without wronging any one. No one can appreciate how much such a friendship means unless it has at one time become a part of his life, nor how keen the sorrow over the unnecessary loss.

Fireside Fancies

Unkind slurs are forever being cast upon these and all other true comradeships. Between man and man they wonder what it is he is trying to gain, between woman and woman what can be her object, but between man and woman there is but one cruel verdict. Such remarks come only from those who have never known what true friendship means ; from those who from their own experience realize how much comfort and happiness it brings come only sympathetic thoughts and joy that to another also has come this great blessing.

One does not admit many such to the inner recesses of the heart, three or four at the most, perhaps only one, but for all the world is an added tenderness because of these quiet friendships that tranquillize and soothe by their very existence.

Close and frequent intercourse is not at all necessary to keep alive this feeling. It does not have to be fanned into a flame by constant assurance that it still exists. Once born it endures for all time. No matter how seldom the interviews, friends

will always meet on the same ground,—
true till the end.

Hasty friendships, so called, often end
in disaster and sorrow.   Real friendship
can come only after years of intercourse,
mutual respect, and a more perfect understanding of the other's character;
formed on so firm a basis the tie is rarely
shattered.   Quick intimacies are as unsatis-
factory as they are unwise, it is much easier
to form than to break them, and when
broken some one is sure to be hurt or
angry, disappointment and bitter feelings
ensue.   But these are not friendships, they
are the natural result of a thoughtless
compact.

Brightness and vivacity attract, may even
hold for a time, but something more is
needed to bind two lives together.   For
the more serious-minded, for those who
look upon life as something more than the
passing of the show, it is not easy to open
the heart and share their inner thoughts
with another; even to those nearest we
cannot give quite all our confidence, some
thoughts are for ourselves alone, they are

felt but never expressed. But it means something worth striving for to gain the love and esteem of men or women who feel their individuality, to whom the *cogito ergo sum* carries a command to use the faculties given them and to bring them to their highest meaning.

Man is a social animal, never at his best alone ; he needs the sympathetic friction of another mind to develop and bring to fruition the possibilities of his nature.

Many become harsh and outwardly disagreeable because they have not been willing, or it may be they have not been able, to let the real beauty of their character show itself. Either from timidity or from too low an estimate of their own worth they permit others to misunderstand and misjudge them cruelly. They suffer keenly from the false position they are forced to occupy, yet are powerless to change it, because they shrink from everything that would savor of a demand for recognition not willingly offered. And so they bear to the end their burden of dreary loneliness. All their lives they have been waiting, longing for the coming of a friend to inspire them with faith, love, and confidence, and a belief in their own capabilities.

AMBITION

" MEN and women make sad mistakes about their own symptoms, taking their vague uneasy longings sometimes for genius, sometimes for religion; and oftener still for a mighty love."

It is, indeed, a sad condition to be in, this transitory state of unsettled longing. The desire to do and to be more than we at present are, not knowing just what it is we do want or what we are capable of doing. Most of us are ambitious, but ambitious for what? That what is just the thing we do not know, the rock on which so many come to grief.

If there were no ambition the age of progress would cease, the world would remain where it is, or, more likely still, retrograde.

Fireside Fancies

It is ambition rightly directed that brings benefits to mankind. But prior to the steady working out of a train of ideas, is the season of discontent, of striving, longing after an intangible something ; in that time of ignorance lies the danger of wrecking one's life by misdirecting the faculties.

No one can do good and efficient work unless his whole heart is in that work. Much valuable force has been wasted by wrongly directed energy.

Without ambition life is colorless, and yet, perhaps, as far as real content goes, people who are satisfied to remain as they are may be happier than their more ambitious neighbors. But do they get as much out of life ? True ! ambitious people are seldom happy people ; but if their failures bring more grief, their successes bring in equal proportion more satisfaction, spurring them on to still greater efforts.

Every one should have a career in life ; few things are more hopelessly depressing than an absolutely aimless existence ; the living from day to day with no thought, no object ahead, is slow murder of brain and body.

The career need not necessarily be one of a public nature, it need only be known and recognized by the individual interested. A course of study, either of books or of humanity, the cultivation of a talent or an effort to help along just one other human being. The calling need not be so great or so glorious that the world will look on and applaud. To few are given a genius that can command the admiration and respect of a people so hard to please in the way of greatness as are those of the present time ; we are used to wonders ; it takes a very marvel to attract unusual attention to-day.

But whether the calling be great or small, let it be something, some object of paramount interest ; the days will seem shorter and pleasanter and life will have a zest quite unknown to those who live merely because they breathe and so are obliged to pass the hours in some way.

It is the "vague uneasy longings" that bring such discomfort and sorrow. A fixed purpose is the staff to rely upon to help us along over the stony road of ambition.

Men attribute these longings to a multitude of things ; with women the scope is narrower, generally confined to one of two things, love or religion, both dangerous, unless they are a natural part of one's life, developing without our being conscious that a foreign element is at work within us ; whichever one is rashly encouraged will be too apt to go to extremes, doing good to none and, it may be, harm to many. For the majority a normal state of existence is safest.

Young people are oftenest the victims of these mysterious aspirations. They are overwhelmed with a feeling of unrest, a desire for something to which they cannot put a name. Life becomes humdrum and wearisome in its monotony until the something takes form and becomes animated with life.

This is a speculative age, and speculation is a dangerous play. Unless one has the desire backed by ability to start at the very beginning and go clear through a subject, it is much wiser to keep aloof altogether, for

> " A little learning is a dangerous thing ;
> Drink deep, or taste not the Pierian spring :
> There shallow draughts intoxicate the brain,
> And drinking largely sobers us again."

Speculative philosophy as put forth in popular novels is responsible for much of the unrest found among the younger element. These half-propounded theories and vaguely suggested ideas do little harm to people of settled purpose, who have learned to think for themselves and reason out matters according to their own philosophy or orthodoxy ; but for the mind just learning to think, eager for new ideas, yet not capable of extracting the good from the bad, the right from the wrong, they are dangerous and unsettling, giving false ideas of life, clothing in mystery the simple beauty of living a Godlike life. To destroy a faith is only too easy, to restore it is next to impossible. But ambition can easily surmount the spirit of unrest implanted by these or any other causes ;

honest, manly ambition can bring to us all life has to offer; without it man is on a level with the beast; with vices added he had better never have been.

The ambition which crushes all in the way of its fulfilment, using its fellow-mortals merely as so many tools while they may serve its purpose, casting them aside as useless and troublesome incumbrances as soon as the end is gained, is an ambition unworthy the name, a misnomer; call it rather a vanity, that is a more fitting term. No ambition is a worthy one unless the means employed to reach the end are strictly honorable. Men had better remain on the animal level, obscure but respected, rather than gain such dizzy heights where the world is looked down upon from the piled-up misery of humanity that has been trodden down in the pathway of the un-scrupulous aspirant for power. Such brilliant comets as Napoleon leave mourning, desolation, and ruin in their track; and all for the glory of one human atom.

Power is a dangerous agent, few are wise enough to use it well.

THE FIRST SNOW

FEW are utterly indifferent to the first
snow-storm of the season. With most it
causes a feeling of jollity and is suggestive
of all sorts of pleasant things.

Sleigh-bells tinkle in our ears, sleds go
whizzing past our mental visions, snow-
balls break with a gentle, almost caressing
thud against our backs, skates skim along
over the ice, cutting all sorts of fancy
figures on its smooth surface. Christmas
greens, bulging stockings, Santa Claus,
candy-pulls, ghost stories told before the
blazing logs while a gruesome blackness
and silence pervade the rest of the room.
Pumpkin-head lanterns and snow-men all
jumbled together in one delightful confusion. All this is in the country, of course,
where snow belongs. In the cities it is
sadly out of place, a fact which it seems to
realize, for it makes haste to disappear as
quickly as possible.

The first snow ! With what rapture it is

hailed by all the small men and women ! What frolics await them, mimic battles where the snow cannon-balls cause the air to vibrate with shouts of merriment rather than echo the groans of the dying which follow a volley of the sterner stuff ! And then the sledding ! There is hardly a boy in the world but has something which by courtesy can be called a sled. What fun it is to glide along so smoothly over the hard, glistening roads pulled by the other fellow ! It will be your turn next to do the pulling, but never mind that, it is almost as much fun to pull as to be pulled, and very soon the long coasting hill will be reached where no motive power is needed ; one wee little push to the sled and off it goes, rushing headlong down the long, smooth track that stretches out safely before it. To be sure, it is not quite so much fun to toil up again to the top as it is to glide so easily down to the bottom, and it takes about five times as long, for that swift descent is over almost before they realize it has begun. The ascent is laboriously accomplished, two steps back for

The First Snow

every one gained, but the summit is reached at last, and throwing themselves face downward on the gayly painted sleds, off they rush again, these happy, rosy, laughing boys and girls. They work hard, although they call it play, for they know this kind of fun will be over all too soon, for the snow has a way of vanishing that is most aggravating to country children, and they mean to make the most of it while it does last.

And for the children of a larger growth it has its fascination also. How silently they fall, these tiny flakes of white, which multiply so fast, soon covering trees, hedges, and lawns with a garment of softest down ! Not a sound to be heard, nature as well as man seems hushed into silence, gazing with awe upon this miracle which in a few short hours so changes the aspect of all things. Beautiful, spotlessly pure. Oh ! the pity of it that we become so accustomed to such sights that we look upon them with indifference or, worse still, grumble because it makes the walking bad. Put on high rubber shoes so you will not mind how deep the snow is, and go out into it and feel the flakes against your cheek, watch the myriad forms they assume as for one instant they rest upon the black background your coat gives them.

There is a sense of exhilaration about walking in a country snow-storm that to a lover of nature is positively intoxicating. Look at that sloping hill-side where the brown earth is fast disappearing under the fleecy covering, look at the trees as they stand outlined against this curtain of white with each branch and tiny twig so sharply defined, forming a very net-work of lace in their graceful tracery. The little stream below still ripples along in its course ; Jack Frost has not been abroad long enough yet to silence the music of its voice, but he soon will be, for he is drawing nearer and nearer, borne on by the fleet wings of the north wind, and soon the little stream will become a smooth mirror for nature to look upon and enjoy the reflection of her own beautiful self.

But now the silent snow is turning into sharp little bits of sleet, and we are per-

force obliged to hurry home, back to the
cosey fireside. These stinging pin-pricks
are very different from the tender, caressing kisses upon eyes, hair, and lips of the
dainty, fairy snow. We shudder to think
of the distance between here and the bright
warmth that awaits us, and almost wish we
had not come quite so far; almost, but not
quite, for the beauty and pleasure of the
outward walk will more than compensate
for the trudge back.

And to-morrow, if the sun shines, a
veritable fairy-land will surround us. Alad-
din's palace with all its glittering jewels
will sink into insignificance in comparison
with this scene before us, every tree and
bush, even the commonest fence-rail, will
be glorified, covered with countless flashing
diamonds, rubies, and sapphires, dancing,
sparkling in the sunlight with a splendor
too great for poor earthly eyes to endure.

" For every shrub, and every blade of grass,
   And every pointed thorn seemed wrought in glass ;
   In pearls and rubies rich the hawthorns show,
   And through the ice the crimson berries glow ;

Fireside Fancies

The thick-sprung reeds, which watery marshes yield,
Seem polished lances in a hostile field;
The stag in limpid currents with surprise
Sees crystal branches on his forehead rise ;
The spreading oak, the beech, the towering pine,
Glazed over in the freezing ether shine ;
The frightened birds the rattling branches shun,
Which wave and glitter in the distant sun,
When, if a sudden gust of wind arise,
The brittle forest into atoms flies,
The crackling wood beneath the tempest bends,
And in a spangled shower the prospect ends."

BOOKS

WHAT would humanity do without books, the source of so much knowledge, recreation, and pleasure ?

From our first acquaintance with Mother Goose, whoever that world-famous lady was, —and it is not improbable that some day the investigating minds of the theorists may settle that question also for us as satisfactorily as they have many another ; but be that as it may, all honor to her name, at one time in his life she has been the joy of every child's heart, and many a mother has had cause to be thankful to her,—from our earliest knowledge of those charming nonsense rhymes, we pass through stage after stage in literature until the highest grade is reached, that being determined according to each individual capacity.

In the choice of books for children one cannot be too particular, for when the mind is just opening it is most susceptible to impressions, and once received they are not easily effaced. To the juvenile mind the printed page is infallible, and carries far greater weight than do the same words spoken by parent or friend. Largely in accordance with the books read is the mental growth. Particularly is this the case with those of vivid imaginations. Boys after reading tales of wild and heroic incidents are consumed with the desire to go out into the world in search of adventures, which are always to end in fame and a return at last loaded with riches and honors. A girl at the same period of her career reads sentimental novels, cries her eyes out over the tribulations and sorrows of the wishy-washy heroine ; mopes around the house for days looking woe-begone and dejected, and coaxes herself into the belief that her life is fearfully dull and prosaic, and that she is not understood by her family, who cannot appreciate the supersensitive refinement of her nature.

However, both boy and girl outgrow this class of literature, and in time look back with an indulgent smile over the follies of their youth.

There are so many books and so short a time in which to read them, that it is well-nigh hopeless to decide which one of them all we most desire to take up next. It is literally an embarrassment of riches. Whatever the taste of the reader may be, there is a wide field from which to choose. To those already written many new ones are added, each month making the selection a more and more difficult matter.

Just at this time the socialistic novel (for so it might be ranked) claims the attention of many men of many minds. Each book of this sort deals more or less effectively with the all-engrossing topics of the day. Each one, it is to be supposed, has some object in view, perhaps the righting of the wrong which has given a theme to the book ; but they are, as a rule, of a highly sensational character, and frequently run to such violent extremes that it is a question whether they even help to accomplish the desired reform. For books, like people, must work slowly, with the greatest care, limitless patience, and infinite tact, in order to be able to overcome evil.

With many of the younger element there is a growing tendency toward a more solid style of reading than the ordinary novel can furnish ; from it they turn to light essays, books of travel, or to some of those delightful historical romances of which a past generation has made us heirs.

But to become familiar with the masterminds of all ages requires preparation ; little by little the mind must be educated to be able to receive comprehensively what they have to give. One must have an understanding of life and his own relation to the world at large. Not until then will the full meaning of such books be clear to him. That which before he was utterly unable to understand he will now feast upon ; each sentence will open a new door in his mind.

A volume filled with earnest thoughts and pure aspirations cannot fail to exert an unconscious influence for good over the most frivolous person. Some gain must follow. As the taste becomes educated the mental palate demands better and stronger food, until gradually it will assimilate only the best. When others fail us our books are the companions to whom we turn for comfort and consolation ; sure always of finding in them the same stanch, true friends. They amuse us when we are weary or dull, soothe us when troubled ; and often they offer some sound little bit of philosophy or advice that makes us ashamed of the weakness we have permitted to master us. With renewed courage come other and more successful efforts, the result of that trying again which has solved great problems and brought civilization to its present degree of enlightenment.

For the stay-at-homes there is always a delightful pleasure in taking up a well-written volume of travels ; soon oblivious

to all surroundings, to be transported hundreds of miles away, journeying through
new regions, drinking in the marvellous
creations of nature and enjoying the quaint
sights and sounds of other nations. A
book of this kind is next best to seeing
and hearing with one's own eyes and ears.
Without fatigue one is able to wander
wherever the fancy wills, crossing oceans,
climbing mountains, or creeping, scarce
daring to breathe, along the jagged edge
of some steep precipice. Or we are in
flowery far-off Japan, gazing in delighted
admiration at the odd, interesting life of
these smiling, courteous people who have
proved their ability in so many directions,
and not least in their appreciation of the
benefits to be derived from a civilization
which can only be the result of a free
and liberal education of men and women
alike.

And so we journey on and on, scaling
the highest Alps or threading the dreary
passages of the Catacombs, now and
then running into some startling bit of
history which makes us shudder with

horror and turn the page hastily on the
recital of man's deeds of wickedness and
tyranny which for the self-glory of one
individual has caused the misery of whole
nations.

Were it not for books how little any one
could know in one short lifetime about this
wonderful world and wonderful time in
which we live! As long ago as 1344
Richard de Bury, Bishop of Durham, said
of them, "They are the masters who in-
struct us without rods and ferules, without clothes or money. If you approach
them, they are not asleep; if investigating
you interrogate them, they conceal nothing; if you mistake them, they never
grumble; if you are ignorant, they cannot
laugh at you. The library, therefore, of
wisdom is more precious than all riches,
and nothing that can be wished for is
worthy to be compared with it." If this
were true more than five centuries ago,
what an infinitely greater weight the same
truth carries to-day! A quarter of the
Christian era lies between the time the
good bishop lived and wrote and we who

have such easy access to all the learning
that came before and has become a part
of the earth's heritage since. How mea-
gre must his library have been, even with
all its beautifully illuminated manuscripts,
in comparison with our own well-filled
shelves !

It would be impossible now to realize a
time when there was no Shakespeare, no
Milton, no Scott, no Dickens, and dozens
of others whose names are on the lips of
every child. Few of the humblest homes
are without these household gods. Their
characters are better known and almost as
real as the more substantial men and
women of flesh and blood who, known to-
day are forgotten to-morrow, but they, like
the gods of old, are immortal. Who could
imagine a Rosalind or a Juliet grown old
and feeble, indifferent alike to love and
all that makes life worth living? Does
any one have to be told who Meg Mer-
rilies was ? The very name of Uriah Heep
causes a shudder of disgust as we thrust
from our mind all thought of the cringing
creature with his cold, clammy hands, and

for the poor little crooked doll's dress-
maker we wipe away a furtive tear even
while on our lips hovers a tender smile.

For the knowledge so easily acquired
through the medium of books can one be
sufficiently grateful? A few weeks of
careful reading gives to us the result of
years of laborious study and earnest re-
search. On whatever subject we may
desire information, whether in science,
archæology, philosophy, or in a thousand
other directions, already the field has been
explored and ably commented upon for
the benefit of those who have not the
opportunities nor perhaps the ability to
make so thorough a study for themselves. Within the covers of half a dozen
carefully selected volumes may be found
material sufficient to familiarize one's self
with almost any subject.

BOOKS AND PEOPLE

In the great race for gain' tis frequently
in the sordid sense only that it is considered,
but if carried to excess the pursuit of the
dollar dwarfs the ability as well as the desire for gain of another kind, the intellectual and moral, which makes of minor
importance the other sort of gain, necessary as that is for the well-being of man.
Granting that he already possesses training,
without it his wealth, whether counted by
thousands or by millions, will be more
likely to prove a curse than a blessing, not
to himself only, but to others also.

It is to these other kinds of gain that
the success most worth attaining is attributable. The moral gain gives stability
and fixity of character, the mental, purpose,
and the intellectual augments and develops
the other two, thus creating that perfect
trinity which makes the human being other
than the brute beast. With the development of these is evolved the creature man

79

was meant to become. Social environment, the many wearisome annoyances and
trials, the hard, bitter facts that daily beset
us, all are rendered easier to endure and
to overcome by carefully looking after the
trinity of gains.

But to these three a fourth must be
added, for the physical gain is of equal
importance. Without health it is a difficult
matter to keep the mind strong and vigorous, for that as well as the body may easily
become diseased. All pursuits then become a labor, the results of which will be
as warped, unsound, and unhealthy as the
poor overwrought body and brain from
which they sprung. True, there have been
a few brilliant exceptions, but exceptional
in a measure only ; their genius has been
morbid, often distorted, rendered interesting, perhaps, only because of its weird con-
ceptions. Therefore the training and care
of each separate gain is equally important.

Too much pains or thought cannot be
given to the formation of mind and character, or too much consideration to the
many elements that contribute to the in-

fluence that surroundings have upon the
individual.

In the lives of the majority, people and
books are the most influential factors in
determining events and guiding the course
of affairs. Both have contributed in large
measure toward the finished product,—
adult man. From each associate one has
the right to expect and demand much that
will contribute to the general welfare.
And as one of the people much is expected
from each one of us, and much must be
given. Not in personal intercourse alone
but through whatever channel is possible.

If one has the ability to express himself
in writing, let him try, and do his best in
that way also, for a book to be known and
loved need not necessarily be the work of
genius, it need only be human to appeal
to the heart, and may be a treasured possession in many a household where the
author himself is but a name only. If,
then, the book and the individual are con-
ceded to be the two most important elements in the development of man, from
which has most been gained? Does the

passivity of the one or the vital personality of the other most affect us?

From those by whom we are surrounded and live in daily intercourse, and from the friends whose warm hand-clasps and loving glances denote the bonds of sympathy which hold our lives together, something is constantly being given out, some influence imbibed. Even from those outside people, —strangers whom we meet to greet, only to sever and then part eternally. They, too, have something to offer.

As these strange people come into our lives they sometimes leave an indelible mark upon the character. By a word or an action they have suggested something different, have brought the next round of the ladder a little nearer, have left behind them an inspiration and awakened ambition, without which life is colorless indeed ; hopelessly depressing, the weary routine of days drag themselves heavily along, adding one after another to their number, taking one more from the span of life, but adding nothing to life itself; leaving nothing accomplished,—nothing done.

Books and People

The spark of ambition must be dormant in every nature, needing only the congenial fire of a kindred spirit to set it aglow, for man is a social animal and requires human sympathy to enable him to give freely of his best and truest. The recluse may excite admiration and wonder by the depths of his thought, the creations of his fancies. But it is only admiration ; the world cannot live by his theoretical ideas, true though they may be, for a truth to be useful must be animated with life ; it can then be incorporated with the unwritten laws which govern the universe ; until then it lacks that one essential touch which makes all humanity akin ; their authors have been apart from, not of the people, they have written from the stand-point of what ought to be rather than what is. To understand the practical needs of one's fellows it is necessary to live in close communion with human-kind.

From the passing throng we gather up bits by the way and stow them safely in the storehouse of memory, from whence they sometimes rise to confront us with stern and frowning menace when we fancied them lying forgotten covered over with the dust of oblivion. These unwelcome but wholesome reminders come from a source not to be escaped, giving to thoughts and actions their right names, their real motives, never once glossing them over with the courteous excuses our willing ears are too ready to accept.

Is it, then, from the living breathing people of to-day that most is gained, or from those dead and gone ones with whom books give us intercourse ?

Many an old philosopher has left behind him a rich legacy of thought, and from those of a less stoical creed we learn of life's joys and æsthetics. They tell us of men and women who lived and loved thousands of years ago in an era of magnificence and sybaritish luxury that is positively dazzling to practical nineteenth century eyes. They were surrounded by that excess of elegance which the experience of many nations has proved to be so enervating. It made of these stern warriors and silver-tongued orators playthings

of the hour, warping their judgment, be-
numbing their faculties, blinding them to
the difference between right and wrong,
causing them to lose their manly vigor and
courage and to become in time mere puppets in the hands of their enemies. And the
women of these times ? It is a sad truth to
say that few among them were pure ; virtue
and the attributes of noble womanhood,
wifehood and motherhood, were well-nigh
unknown. What wonder that under such
demoralizing circumstances empires crum-
bled and fell ! Again and again they rose
Phœnix-like from their ashes only to again
be consumed, until now a saner people has
arisen, and law and order have taken the
place of personal license.

From such phases of degraded humanity
it is a relief to turn to a purer people whose
aspirations are higher, who at least strive
to be men and women.

Through the magic door-way of book-
lore any age, any clime can be entered.
In a moment we can be in the midst of interesting people, or beautiful scenes lie un-
folded before the mental vision. Thoughts

are suggested profound and learned, subtle and exquisite, requiring from us only that we be receptive ; much or little can be gained according as the mind has been trained.

Yet, after all, necessary as books are with their never-ending fund of entertainment, fascinating knowledge, and earnest thought, is it not the human sympathy we are most in need of, the warm hand-clasp, the quick glance of sympathy that assures us we are understood, the close personal intercourse ? These mean more than all the books that ever were written. One can live without books, but without love it is a cold and dreary world indeed.

Our library friends are ever the same, we know just where to find them, in just what mood they will be, and which one of them will appeal to us most at the time, to which the mind is best attuned. Not so with those other friends, who like ourselves are ever struggling to make the real and the ideal harmonize. Of them we are not quite so sure, in the exchange of ideas we must be ever on the alert lest we be caught napping, there is an agreeable consciousness of the friction of one mind upon another; always anxious to understand no less than to be understood, one feels alive, a part of the moving universe. This personal intercourse spurs one on in the desire to make and hold a worthy position in the front ranks where integrity and honor hold sway.

The same ideas derived from the printed page are sneered at as pedantic, considered Utopian, very pretty but quite impracticable in this work-a-day world. A harsh comment surely on human nature when what is manly and true is not useful in every-day life!

So it is, perhaps, the actors on the stage of to-day who have the most influence upon the daily lives of their fellows. Still, it is an open question whether from them the gain is of the greatest good or from the now mute voices of those who live only through the books they have bequeathed to successive generations.

AUTHORSHIP

To be a successful author means one of two things, either great genius or the power of sensationalism ; which is the more popular must be decided by the people. The former is read by a few, the latter, at this time, perhaps at all times, by the many ; therefore it would seem that the highest meed of praise must be reluctantly accorded to one who makes our flesh creep, the cold perspiration bespangle our intellectual brows, and the dark to be peopled with unknown terrors to our disordered visions.

The sensational and realistic writers have, it is true, but a passing reputation. Their names, famous to-day, are forgotten to-morrow, while real genius lives forever. But geniuses are few, and growing fewer it would seem, while the popular writer we have ever with us ; he is all-pervading, everlasting. When one particular star sets there are dozens of new ones to take his place and shed their light for the benefit of mankind.

But of the thousands of books published every year how many make their author's name known beyond a very limited circle? It is a pathetic tale they would have to tell, the most of them, could they speak: of the animation and vigor with which they were begun when first the divine spark was felt by the aspirant for literary honors; how the words fairly jostled each other in his eagerness to put on paper these thoughts which seemed to him so full of meaning, which were to convey a message to the world. How feverishly he wrote fearing some part might escape his untutored memory. How thought chased thought when once the impetus was given, until in the chaos of ideas he was fain to fling his pen to the floor in utter despair of ever bringing into anything like system this unruly mass of matter; but with perseverance order is at length restored and the work continued. What moments of anxiety he endured in the great desire to make plain to others what to himself was

so clear, or, if the book was a novel, to
make situation, incident, and conversation
striking and original. For a time all went
well and the work progressed rapidly, then
followed a time of inaction when the brain
utterly refused to perform its duty ; not an
idea came ; the poor author was hopelessly
stranded.

For most authors literature is not like
other enterprises, so much work to be
gotten through each day, but it must be
done when the brain wills ; be it little or
much, the time necessary to accomplish it
must be given. As to those authors who
when asked about their method of working reply that they give just so many
hours each day to their literary labors or
write so many lines or words, never ex-
ceeding that limit, it may be all very well,
but it is to be doubted if there is much
true genius about it. Hack work could
readily be done in such a way, but the
books that have lived for centuries past
and will go ringing on through those to
come, the books that one can live by, were
they written so many words at a time?

Emphatically, no. A great thought must be expressed at once or it may be lost forever.

But of the books that do not live, those hundreds and thousands of volumes that come so fresh and crisp from the printer's hands to take their places in melancholy rows along the bookseller's shelves ! With what hopes and fears they have been given up by their authors to an unsympathetic public, these children of the brain ! To their creators at least they have meant much, have been held dear. When the first proof-sheet is sent home, with what pride is it surveyed, how carefully read to correct any typographical error that may occur, and then returned to the publisher ; what the printers call form has again to be corrected. Finally, the book appears a completed volume, with all the precious ideas held close between the gilded covers. Then the anxious author begins to scan carefully all periodicals where book reviews are to be found, all papers where he may come upon a criticism of this his first essay in the field of literature. " Hope deferred maketh the heart sick," and truly it is hard to be utterly ignored or damned with faint praise. To be lustily hauled over the coals and pronounced utterly bad is infinitely better, for a critic pronouncing this judgment on a book is sure to make it popular for a time at least. People want to see for themselves what it is he has so roundly condemned, and so the book rejoices in a short-lived popularity. Better that than absolute oblivion? Perhaps, but to be loved for a day and then flung away, it may be, is harder than never to have been loved at all.

But failure is never popular, so enough of books that do not live, of disappointed hopes. The successful *literati* are the envied ones of earth, how they outshine the lesser lights in the firmanent! They are courted and lionized to their heart's content, and delight in the popular adulation. He who does not desire praise must be more than human, even the most confirmed cynic is susceptible to flattery. But Dame Fortune is fickle, she waves even the biggest lion aside with, Enough, make way. A

newer light has flashed upon her vision.
Le roi est mort, vive le roi!

In reviewing the celebrated men and
women of the world's history, it is those
who have been renowned for their intellectual gifts who hold the highest and best
places. Great warriors, famous statesmen,
step aside and bow before genius, kings
and queens look up to and revere intellect.
Where Plato sits there is the head of the
table.

To take a more prosaic view of the subject, is literature a paying profession?

It would seem not, few authors are rich,
from their books, at least. Has it not become proverbial that genius lives in an
attic? And have not these very attics become shrines whither the devout pilgrim
from all civilized lands journeys to offer his
homage? With what reverent feet we
tread the ground where Thoreau's hut once
stood by lovely Walden pond! our voices
hushed as if we feared the very birds to
pause in their flight and chide us for dis-
respect. Not far from the one time home
of this philosophic dreamer is a quiet

country graveyard embowered in trees, tall,
stately oaks and graceful elms wave their
branches in silent benediction over the quiet
dead sleeping so calmly their long sleep.
Hidden away among the green loveliness
on a sloping hill-side is a small white marble
stone not more than a foot square ; it contains but one word, "Hawthorne," but
that is enough. What a host of memories
it brings up of this man who left his
clerk's desk at the old custom-house in
Salem to go out and become immortal !
Not many yards away, in the full glare of
the sunlight, are imposing granite shafts
extolling the virtues of those who lie beneath, but who gives them a second glance ?
Genius needs no monument of stone to
keep its memory alive.

Can it be that the man of genius is so
often poor because he is somewhat one-
sided in his nature ? To gain riches practical good sense is required, and practicality
is generally just what he lacks ; he feels that
his mission in life is much too valuable to
waste time in the pursuit of anything that
does not relate to the one, all-absorbing

subject. Few among them are what may be termed all-round individuals ; they have let their one absorbing idea become so a part of themselves, have become so one with it, as to almost totally exclude the more homely but necessary side of life, and so little by little they have let matters take care of themselves, until there is nothing left to take care of ; then comes the heart-breaking struggle with poverty, which so often ends in the downfall and complete annihilation of a brilliant mind. The physical man cannot starve and yet keep the mental man alive. The want of and struggle for daily bread has cost the world dear in the loss of talent crushed by cruel necessity.

NOVELS

SINCE Richardson started a new era in novel writing down to the latest scribbler for the penny dreadful, almost without exception the heroines of these more or less thrilling tales have been made beautiful ;

even the type of beauty has not varied to any great extent. It is either a face and form which seem all too ethereal to inhabit this coarse earth, or else the lady is a beauty whose cheeks glow with health, whose cherry lips meet to kiss each other over rows of priceless pearls, and whose eyes, like twin stars, sparkle with merriment or grow liquid with meaning when the tender heart is touched with sympathy for another.

A little florid this description? Well, perhaps so; but one need not turn over the pages of many novels before finding its counterpart.

But if the type of beauty has changed so little since the time of the parent of the novel, by no means can the same thing be said of the style of the heroines, the fragile Cecilias and Clarissas who sat demurely at their embroidery-frames while mamma entertained the guests, and who promptly fainted on all and every occasion that required the least action or presence of mind. But after all, what mattered it! for the lover always appeared in the most opportune way to carry off the adored one in his arms to a place of safety; when on opening her eyes she finds him bending over her in deep solicitude, she, like a well-brought-up maiden should do, faints again at finding herself in so indecorous a position.

What a change from the proper and sedate heroines our grandmothers wept and smiled over to the strong-minded, athletic young women who adorn the pages of the novel of to-day!

It is just possible a happy medium might be struck, indeed, very often has been, by the writers of a fast passing generation. But the novelist of this day in order to be read must be up to date. So his heroine is strong-minded, of socialistic tendencies, an ardent advocate of the white ribbon, a doctor, a lawyer, or whatever else may happen to be the fad most in vogue at the time.

But of whatever cult they may be, what they have looked upon and desired to be their life's work, all that ends for them when Cupid bends his bow and they are dragged willing victims to the altar of Hymen, the goal of life, so the novelists would have us believe, and surely they ought to know, for it is life they seek to depict.

Now, how refreshing it would be if somebody would write a story whose heroine did not put to the blush by her virgin loveliness the freshly awakened dawn, whose hero was an ordinary man, and where no subtle villain, under the guise of their best friend, sought to bring disaster and ruin to all! If such a remarkable volume did appear, possibly it might not prove so absorbingly interesting as pages dark with crime and the timely frustration of it by the guardian angel of the pair. But then from its very novelty it might prove a hit. A book in which a plain Hannah or Martha (not a bit romantic names) should have her love and adventures narrated. For even plain Hannahs and Marthas, not only plain but sometimes decidedly homely, do have their loves and adventures. Sad, indeed, were it if all the sugar-plums of life fell into the lap of spoiled beauty. Very often it is these outwardly less attractive daughters of Eve who draw the biggest prizes in the everlasting lottery of living.

Novels

But the world loves beauty, and as they say all women are beautiful in the eyes of those who love them, perhaps that is the reason that the creators of these several types of heroines have really found them beautiful to their inner sight, so hasten to present them in fitting guise to the public. It is a generally accepted theory that love is blind, so very likely they only show them as they themselves fancy them to be.

But a distinctly ugly heroine would be a relief to be hailed with delight, especially if she was just an ordinary, every-day girl, who neither sang like an angel nor painted like a Titian. Just an ordinary girl who was lovable because of her sweet womanliness.

But enough of heroines. They are all so much alike that any further description would prove trite.

Novels to be read must be interesting. They must be either extremely good, extremely bad, or very much *à la Zola.* Those which do not come under any of these headings soon find a grave in cold oblivion. It is hard for the authors, no doubt, to see these children of their brain so cavalierly dealt with, but the good of the many must be considered before that of the few, and in this way the much-enduring public is saved from one affliction at least.

Dialect stories so much in vogue at the present time are laboriously read, and said to be enjoyed. No doubt many of them are wonderfully good, but one can only guess at the meaning of half the words. Why write for a public in a language it cannot understand? Breathe it not aloud, but can it be another fad?

And then those stories, written for the upper crust, but whose characters savor strongly of beer and onions, whose conversation in Bowery lingo is freely sprinkled with pure Saxon oaths. What such people say and do is often very much to the point, and a rough exterior may clothe a noble mind, but truly it is a harsh comment on human nature when such efforts of genius are greedily devoured and become the *on dit* of the day by men and women whose position would suggest that home truths conveyed in the language of refinement would seem to be the natural medium of communication.

Realism is entering very largely, perhaps too much so, in the life and writings of the time. If some things were unfit to talk about and write about a quarter of a century ago, does not the same hold good to-day? There was a strong revulsion to Puritanical ideas following the too broad period that preceded it. The time would again seem to be not far distant when another movement of the kind, a modified one at least, might not be inopportune.

There are few novels and dramas now before the public which do not leave behind them just a little uncomfortable feeling, a wish that something had been left out.

The minute descriptions of crimes, so largely indulged in by some authors, has undoubtedly helped many a less clever villain to the successful working out of his schemes. Were it not for the detailed minutiæ of detective stories, there might not be so many prisoners at our docks, and such dangerous ones. The educated villain who is clever enough to escape detection does infinitely more harm than the clumsy bungler, who is sure to be caught after two or three attempts, and is then shut up out of harm's way for a time.

In really good novels what is conveyed between the lines means often much more than the printed words themselves. A sentence here, a paragraph there, and this book is forgotten as one's mind wanders off into a train of ideas suggested by what has just been read. It is a delightful way of reading, and causes a pleasant sense of one's own cleverness as thought chases thought through the brain.

Books, like people, should not be all on the surface; they should be loved better as we learn to know them better.

IMAGINATION VERSUS FACTS

Hamilton Mabie has called imagination the power that liberates. And surely it does liberate in the freest possible manner from the petty cares and annoyances that continually beset the path of the ordinary mortal. Once give rein to the imagination, and all sense of present surroundings is lost in the delicious abandon that takes possession of one.

Imagination versus facts. The two are more closely allied than a first thought would suggest, for often it is but imagination in the beginning which becomes facts in the end, and such facts as have power to influence the world's history.

Had it not been for the so-called vagaries of the imagination, where would a thousand and one of the to-day's necessities have come from?

Fancy what reception Morse's first indistinct ideas concerning the telegraph would have met with had he even so much as hinted at the possibility of a message being carried hundreds of miles without other aid than that of a small instrument at either end of a thin copper wire; how his suggestion would have been scorned and himself looked upon as a harmless lunatic! But he kept his precious secret until he was able to give practical demon-

strations with satisfactory results, and now
the entire civilized world is his debtor.

From the wizards of our own day, Edison
and Tessla, the marvels that have resulted
from their fancies are something utterly
beyond the comprehension of the ordinary
mind.

Little did Benjamin Franklin guess while
he was enduring the jeers of the small boys
of a hundred years ago that such results
would follow his experiments with the
lightning.

Facts are useful, very necessary to the
routine of living, but without the fancies
of the imagination many of the facts would
remain unborn.

It is the imagination very largely that
makes life endurable for some poor wretches,
whose daily trials would prove more than
they could bear were it not for the power
that liberates, permitting them, for a time at
least, an existence of their own making.
Even mere babies will find happiness for
hours at a time in playing with a bit of
string or an empty spool, fancying them all
sorts of things that please the wee mind,

and from their own little thoughts will be born playfellows whose unseen presence bring far more satisfaction than the more substantial article of flesh and blood; often these little friends become so real to them that it is almost with difficulty they can realize they are but names only. There are many instances of children keeping these same imaginary comrades as a very real part of their lives for months and sometimes even years.

With advancing time these childish fancies take the form of more ambitious dreams. It is then one begins to acquire real estate within the borders of sunny Spain.

But it is not always that these dreams assume form sufficiently to become accepted facts; many worthy to rank among the world's treasures have remained the unshared property of him to whom the dream has come, and his alone because of his inability to put into words the thought which is so exquisitely subtle as to prove altogether elusive when any attempt is made to express it in a language too coarse to con-

vey its finely shaded meaning. Many of
our truest poets are, alas ! silent ones,

" Who die with all their music in them,"

while other many have been able to secure
the jewelled bridle which guides aright the
glorious winged steed. Fancy a poet without imagination ; 'tis as easy to conceive as
of a river without water, the merest mock-
ery of the word. Poets are born, not made.
So it is with imagination ; the attempted
cultivation of either bringing but a dismal
failure as a result.

But he who is blessed with that rare gift
is fortunate, indeed. There are few who
really possess it, for imagination means
something more than the idle fancies that
flit through every brain. It is the cause
of the first suggestion and an ever ready
helper in the working out of all the beauties
that are fashioned by the mind and hand
of man. Without beauty to refine our
surroundings much would be lost and men
and women be little above the animal
level.

Imagine a world without poetry, music,

and art! Yet without imagination to lay the corner-stone any one of these would have been an impossibility. Place a sculptor duly equipped with all the necessary tools before a block of marble, deny him the inspiration born of imagination, then gaze upon the result. The finished figure may be anatomically correct and gracefully posed, but one may look long for any real beauty in it.

The statues of Venus and the Apollo Belvidere were fashioned by no such prosaic individuals. Fancy what visions of ideal beauty were running riot in the brains of their creators while their deft fingers were moulding the willing clay.

True, we could live without beauty, and the divine harmonies of Beethoven are no more necessary to existence than are the glories of an Italian sunset, but who that has once enjoyed either would willingly forego them for the rest of his life! Such sights and sounds bring a sense of keen pleasure that all the necessary facts in Christendom cannot conjure up. They appeal to all the finer instincts in human nature.

Fireside Fancies

But imagination is a greater factor than would be the case if it were only the source of all such useless trash as Mr. Gradgrind considers all things that are not strictly useful and necessary facts connected with the daily doings of life. It is the primary cause of all great inventions. One of the mightiest powers in all the world was evolved from the mind of Heron the Alexandrian about the year 100 B.C. Something suggested to him the force of steam, and from his well-balanced brain, aided by a vivid imagination, came the idea of a machine to be constructed which was to have for its motive power steam. It was constructed and did successfully the work it was intended to perform. And now look at what has resulted from that first vague fancy. That was two thousand years ago. During all those years how many people had watched the steam escaping from a tea-kettle ! yet not until James Watts, only so short a time ago as the latter part of the last century, sat dreaming over the kitchen fire, gazing at the strange antics of the kettle's lid, did it suggest to any one the force which was in a measure to reconstruct and bring about the modern locomotive, that lumbering iron machine which enables us to overcome distances with as much ease as though they did not exist.

Idle imagination, indeed ! a fig for those who scoff, and a sigh of sympathy for those who are denied so great a treasure.

Glorious imagination, productive imagination, one of the richest blessings that can fall to the lot of man, and through him a boon to all the world. Bulwer speaks of it as the arch beautifier of character, that sweet purifier of mere intellect.

⁂

CASTINE

SITTING here in this odorous forest of pines, many hundred feet above one of the most beautiful bays in the world, what calm, serene thoughts come to one as the eye rests upon the scene stretched out at one's feet! this great expanse of water flowing

out to join the ever restless sea. Nothing
in that direction but water,—water blue and
deep as far as the eye can follow it.

But turn away from the horizon toward
the shore, with its bold rocky promontories
crowned with grand old forest-trees. On
the highest point of all the light-house, that
beacon of hope to the weary, shivering
sailor, telling of the warmth and cheer that
await him not far off,—only a short distance
now, once the point is safely rounded, and
once again he will be with wife and little
ones who anxiously await his coming.

To many a wanderer does Dice's Head
Light tell a tale of love and home. It is only
a humble third- or maybe fourth-class light,
but it shines out into the night clear and
bright, doing its duty in its appointed place
with the same noble purpose as those oc-
cupying more prominent places. Their
mission is the same.

Lying between these rocky shores is a
harbor, safe enough and large enough for
the navies of half the world to ride at
ease.

How peaceful and beautiful it looks

now ! this sparkling water dotted here and there with islands big and little. Some with scant herbage clinging desperately to the barren rock, struggling hard to gain a sustenance from the unwilling soil; others, again, covered thick with luxuriant greenery. Some scarce showing above the surface of the water, others rearing themselves many feet into the air. At low tide all sorts of fantastic rock formations are revealed ; but all are marked, the mariner need fear no lurking danger here.

As a background for this are long chains of hills, some almost mountains, blue, and sharply outlined against the clear sky, or, again, misty and indistinct, half hidden in banks of fog ; nearer to are thin lines of mist flitting along, cutting the hills in two. Some are bleak and desolate, others robed in nature's garment of living green. Some make an abrupt plunge into the sea ; their almost perpendicular sides cut into cracks, crevices, and caves deep enough to suggest all sorts of delightful mysteries. Still others, sloping gently down, form a smooth shingle beach where many kinds of sea life are washed ashore and out again with each change of the tide.

And then the water itself! sparkling, dancing in the sunlight, reflecting in its clear depths all the beauty of the world above and the wonderful cloud formations in the sky over all. It does not seem cruel and relentless here as in places elsewhere, eager to clutch and destroy its prey ; but bright and joyous, careless of the passing hours in the happiness of the present. And well it may be, for time does not exist for it. Even in times of storm it seems but half in earnest, more petulant than sullen, ready to break again into smiles at the barest suggestion of fair weather.

Then fancy such a scene at sunset lighted up in a haze of purple and gold glory, bathed as it were in the life-blood of the dying monarch. A scene once witnessed never to be forgotten, changing every minute, revealing another bit of the gorgeous panorama, but only to pass it by and light upon still another, and then to fade away into the dull gray of twilight to reappear wrapt in the softer radiance of moonlight, calm and tranquil in shadow, beautiful beyond words to describe, where the silver orb throws her light from shore to shore.

Out of the darkness into this line of flashing jewels comes a tiny boat, all sails set, drifting along on a breath of breeze, making a picture long to be remembered ; and now a canoe is gliding through, the silent dip of its paddles scarce ruffling the placid surface of the water ; it comes, stays but a moment, and is lost in the darkness beyond.

And now the moon is hidden behind a mass of flying clouds, but only to break forth again in a halo of glory beautifying the most humble objects, smiling down a silent benediction on this quaint little town nestling so close to the water's edge, its quiet streets overarched with elms tall and stately, their branches interlacing, forming a net-work of green to shade the infrequent passer-by.

But not always has it been so calm and dignified as it is to-day. It was once and for many generations the scene of strife and confusion. Remains of military breastworks and forts, in a fairly good state of preservation, meet one at every turn. French, English, and Americans have struggled for the possession of this little town with its commanding position and magnificent harbor, it has been a much-coveted and often fought for prize, from the time of the Tarratine Indians until the early part of this century and the war that once for all freed us from a foreign yoke. Since then peace has come and reigns supreme in this most restful spot. Go where one will in Castine, beauty surrounds one. It is one vast panorama of nature in her most majestic pose. Amid such scenes one is lifted above the trivialities of life, everything seems possible. Here can be found rest and peace, a better understanding of one's self. In such a place come thoughts too deep for utterance, an enjoyment so keen as to be nearly akin to pain. That, it may be, is the feeling of the true poet, for poet he is though his thought cannot find expression. They are the songs that never have been, never will be sung ; to put them into words would rob them of the harmony that makes the heart

throb in a very ecstasy of delight. And
yet from that very intensity of feeling
comes absolute suffering ; many things jar
and grate upon such a nature that to one
of more phlegmatic disposition would be
of no moment, if, indeed, he was even conscious of a discord.

Whether such a supersensitive organiza-
tion is desirable is doubtful ; though the enjoyment is keener, so, also, is the suffering.
Does the one counterbalance the other?

The ordinary surroundings of life are
not poetic ; indeed, in most cases they are
hopelessly prosaic ; wings must be clipped,
Pegasus submit to Bellerophon's bridle.
But once the fancy is given freedom, what
glorious, wide flights it takes ! time and
place have ceased to exist, it runs riot
among all nations, amid all ages, or nar-
rows itself down to one happy hour,• and
lives over and over again the bliss of those
fleeting moments.

Ah ! 'tis hard to be forced back to the
dull realities awaiting the return to earth
and, as doubtless many good people would
say, a little ordinary common sense. Yes,

common sense and educated sense are both necessary to help in the performance of the routine duties of living. Uncommon sense and vivid imaginations are not necessary, but who that is blessed with the possession of one or both would willingly give up either? They bring into one's life a something for which there is no name, that changes the whole face of things. Scoff if you like, you intensely practical people to whom a spade is a spade, but until you learn to see with the eyes of imagination as well as reality you are losing three-quarters of the pleasures of existence.

> " Books in the running brooks,
> Sermons in stones,
> And good in everything."

Yes! a thousand times yes for him who has eyes to see and ears to hear them, but for him who has not, the brook is but the water that turns his mill-wheel, the stones are of use for building cellar-walls, and his surroundings are good only in so far as they are conducive to his comfort. But to

the poet the running brook is a little
world in itself, carrying him with it out and
away to lands not yet marked on any map.

❦❦❦

MEN AND WOMEN

WHEN God created Adam, the man, he
deemed it wise to give to him a helpmate,
and so created Eve, the woman, that they
two might find happiness together.

It is well for men and women to form
close friendships. Each has that something
which the other lacks to help and guide
them both.

The man, if he be worthy of the name,
has a strong, vigorous nature, ability, and
desire to cope with the world, to protect
and care for the woman.

Woman's nature is more subtile, her
every sensibility is more acute, and her instinct, that by which she often judges,
rarely plays her false. For her the battle
of life holds no alluring charms. She
likes better to be sheltered and protected

by man's strength. Thus they form a perfect whole,—are the complement of each other. From the very beginning God has shown that he meant this should be.

The influences to which we are subjected have much to do with forming the character. Going out into the world as a man necessarily must do, he comes in contact with much that is coarse and degrading. The world is a rough place, where nearly all are looking out for number one, trying to push aside those who may chance to stand in the way. Only the strongest and wisest survive. Many sharp corners are encountered that must be rounded off in some way,—in an honest way, of course, but there are so many ways of looking at the same subject ; success comes often through devious paths. Familiarity with such things sometimes breeds indifference. To keep his better nature alive to itself a vital contrast is needed ; he should find it among the women he knows.

Social life as well as the business world has its dark side also. Petty ambitions, unworthy subterfuges, scandals, and intrigues are found as often in the drawing-room as on the exchange.

A man has many temptations to lead him astray, and although it is to be deplored, yet it is scarcely to be wondered at that so often his sensibilities do become blunted. At thirty he shrugs his shoulders and smiles at that which at twenty he would have shrunk from in dismay.

Every woman should be made to realize what a powerful influence she has or could have over every man she knows. She has much to answer for in his attitude toward right and wrong, and, above all, in the light in which he views her own sex. If all women are sacred to him, every action of his life will be regulated by the desire to stand well in their sight.

Nothing is so base, so degrading, as the influence of a bad woman ; nothing which will sooner bring misery, disgrace, and remorse.

When a woman falls, God pity her,— every hand is against her ; not one is held out to save her from herself. No wonder she becomes a desperate outcast. She has nothing to hope for,—there is no possibility of her ever rising above this one sin. One false step, and it were better the grave had closed over her forever. Are the rest of womankind so immaculate, so free from faults, that they can stand secure upon the pillar of purity and point the finger of scorn at this woman whose fault has been her weakness? For the sake of our own mothers and sisters can we not try to raise rather than thrust her deeper into the mire? The woman who fears to lose caste by such acts of humanity must be sadly lacking in character.

Perhaps with all women the moral tone is finer than with men, and for that reason her disgrace is looked upon in a very different light from that accorded her tempter. In the eyes of the world her sin is too black to be condoned. Youth, ignorance, all fail to palliate in the smallest degree her crime in weakly yielding to the cowardly persuasions of the man who knows it is she who will suffer, be disgraced, and eternally condemned, while he can and will walk with head erect, received by all as if his character were spotless as snow. For her are none of the thousand and one excuses offered and accepted for him.

Whose sin is the blacker?—the man's,—he whom most women smile upon indulgently and allow to whisper into their willing ears the sweet nothings of society conversation ; or the woman's,—she whose love has been stronger than her weak, trembling self, from whom we women turn in shuddering horror, holding aside our skirts, dreading lest the merest touch of garments should bring contamination? When such treatment is all we have to accord her, are we entirely blameless in the matter of her ultimate degradation? Have we nothing to answer for in gossip and scandal greedily listened to and passed on?

A woman's personality is far-reaching,—all pervading ; in the atmosphere which surrounds her there is an individuality, a something which belongs to her alone ; and is as is she herself, refined and gentle or coarse and lowering to the moral tone.

Real, disinterested friendship between a

man and a woman is unfortunately rare ; when it does exist it is of much benefit to both. But that miserable old creature Dame Gossip will not let them enjoy the companionship ; many a good friendship has been spoiled by her meddlesome interference. A man does not want to marry every woman he may chance to find worthy of admiration, nor does a woman desire to win the affections of every man who interests her.

In sorrow or in joy man turns to woman for sympathy. It should be her great happiness as well as grave responsibility to give to him her best help and noblest thoughts. Women are quick to divine a man's needs, and he to feel her influence. Many lives have been spoiled by being misunderstood or nagged at continually. If not utterly wrecked they have become callous and indifferent.

It should be the duty of every mother to win the respect and confidence of her son ; having gained this, all women will be honored in his sight because of her.

Many girls, through sheer thoughtlessness and love of what they call fun, teach men to regard them lightly, so forfeiting their respect, something once lost never to be regained. In time these girls come to realize what this means, and to many it brings a feeling of recklessness ; becoming less and less womanly, they become more and more creatures of chance. Whether they rise or fall is a pretty even toss up.

Love growing up between a man and a woman is something absolutely sacred. Yet there are people so thoughtless, nay, more, really vulgar, who seem to consider it a huge joke, the occasion for sly glances and pointed remarks. Such actions are positively degrading. This first love is so beautiful, so pure, the happiness it brings so exquisite, as each realizes it dawning in his own heart, hoping, yet fearing, how it may be with the other. They say a woman is more observant in regard to such matters than a man ; it may be that is so ; at all events she nearly always knows when a man is beginning to have for her something more than a feeling of good comradeship. If she knows she cannot care for him, then she is, indeed, culpable if she permits him to go too far. It is bitterly hard for him to be rejected, and it is humiliating as well.

Happily, the class of girls who consider it something to be boasted of when they can add one more to the list of their proposals is fast passing away.

Probably there never yet was a woman so unattractive but some one found her desirable. If she does not marry it is generally from some good reason of her own rather than because she has not had the opportunity.

Every Jack has his Jill, so they say, yet sometimes they never find each other, and only too often Jack discovers too late he has won the wrong Jill. In that case tact and consideration without end are required to make life endurable.

The very happiest time in all a girl's life is when the man she has selected from out the whole world comes to her and tells her that he loves her. To him she gives her whole soul, believing him everything her heart would have. Happy the woman who can carry with her that belief through all

Men and Women

the years of her married life. Much depends upon herself; it takes more than a
pretty face and graceful manners to hold a
husband's love and admiration. The first
year of the new life is the hardest they will
ever know. The routine of home life brings
out many characteristics quite unnoticed in
the halcyon days of the engagement. Many
things that both have been accustomed to
have to be modified or given up entirely;
some one must give in, and if there is to be
any real comfort in the days to come the
giving up must not be all on one side.

Girls of the present day seldom know
much about the management of a house
and the proper treatment to accord servants. At first they cannot quite realize
why the new home cannot be run in just
the same way as the one they have left;
they fail to understand that few men are
able to begin where their fathers leave off.
If the girl knows little, even less does the
new lord of the manor know of domestic
economy. Under the circumstances it is
not at all strange that so many come to
grief.

Fireside Fancies

There are many women who bring up their daughters with the idea of marriage as the one and only object in life. Instead of fitting them for the responsibilities entailed by the sacred trusts of wifehood and mother-hood, this kind of mother generally sacrifices everything that her daughter may have a good time, relieving her from all duties in the home, sewing for her, mending her clothes, in fact, teaching her to be utterly useless and incapable. Poor, deluded mother, she thinks she is doing her child a kindness, whereas she is inflicting a most grievous wrong upon her. Cares and responsibilities must come into every life. It will be doubly hard for this petted child to have them thrust upon her with no knowledge of how to meet them ; because of her training much needless trouble will come to herself and others. For all this self-sacrifice how is the mother repaid ? what does she get in return ? Very little, it must be confessed, for a girl so reared very naturally becomes selfish and cold ; her brightest and best are kept for the outside world which cares nothing for her, while for those who

love her, for the home circle, she has nothing ; she is never happy unless living in a
whirl of excitement.

What wonder when such women marry,
and the butterfly existence must perforce
come to an end, that the home is made miserable. Their own and their husband's lives
wrecked because of their ignorance of the
real meaning of living.   When complaint
and dissatisfaction is all she can find to talk
about, and when old clothes and an untidy
house become habitual, why should he not
go to the club to escape her querulous
tongue?   Is he altogether to blame if he
seeks in the society of other women what
he should find in his wife ?

Men like the butterflies to amuse them,
to have a good time with *en passant*, but
for the long run the more sober-hued moth
brings the more lasting happiness.   When
a man turns his back upon the worries and
annoyances of business he wants a real
home to come to, with a real woman in it,
who finds her greatest happiness in admin-
istering to his comfort and adding to his
happiness.

WOMEN AND THEIR INTERESTS

CLOTHES, servants, gossip, these are the subjects of conversation supposed to be the exclusive and sole right of women ; they are apparently not credited with the ability to go beyond these confines. Even the newspapers of the day have a column headed "Women's Interests," the paragraphs in which will be found to contain matters of great interest, such as the description of gowns worn by our aspiring countrywomen at some court ceremony, or there will be a condescending word of praise bestowed upon some feminine effort, or it may be a few lines regarding a novelty in fancy work. All such things, rather than the vital questions of the times, are no doubt of paramount interest to women. They ought to be if they are not, for all Christendom insists upon the fact that they are.

There are women's magazines by the dozen filled with the same style of literature, fashions in dress, fashions in wearing the hair, fashions in manners, and almost in morals, as if courtesy and goodness were fads to be put on or discarded according to the whim of the moment.

Whole pages are devoted to homilies on the training of children, how to feed and clothe them, punish or praise them, how to educate and guide their mental development. It is an easy affair, this theoretical training of children, as propounded by the writers of these articles. By following these few simple rules how much trouble might be saved these foolish (?) mothers who take into consideration the individual characters of their children and really believe each must be accorded different treatment, and that the clock-work method is not applicable to all alike !

To the busy woman these magazines should be a mine of wealth ; they tell her how to make over her old black silk, how to dye and press a last year's frock, trim it with half a yard of something costing seventy-five cents the yard, and after a phenomenally small amount of labor she will go forth in a gown which will be the source of wondering envy to all her less practical neighbors. But the enterprising editors of these journals go even farther, they are tireless in their painstaking endeavors to be of assistance to the weaker sex. Not satisfied with telling us how to regulate our behavior and morals, they even go so far as to tell us how to set a dinner-table, who to invite and who not to invite to our social functions. In fact, there should be little left to desire after a careful reading of the pages of these magazines. In addition to the above valuable hints are to be found a few stories, a poem or two, in fact, scraps of almost everything of interest to women. There are, of course, periodicals for the emancipated female also, who would scorn such follies as are supposed to interest her weaker sisters. These journals are of a very different order ; they are intensely progressive. In one of them was found, not long ago, an article on man. The writer took a hopeful view of this poor biped, and thought in time, with careful training, help, and consideration on the part of woman, he might—having a fair

amount of brains—attain at last to some
position and ability in the world. Truly,
it is refreshing to find any one taking such
a cheering view of things in this pessimistic
age.

Women certainly do talk a great deal
about clothes and servants, and gossip is
an actual tonic to some natures. But is
the conversation of men always thoughtful
and instructive? Do they never talk about
affairs distinctly frivolous or worse? There
are many women absolutely vapid ; but is
not the scale pretty evenly balanced?
George Eliot has made Mrs. Poyser say,
"There's no denyin' women are foolish.
God Almighty made 'em to match the
men."

Man has had it all his own way so long
that his ideas and theories of right have
come to be accepted as such. But the
woman of to-day is a new creature : she
has just emerged from her shell of forced
inactivity. If she misuses her liberty and
makes herself ridiculous by going to violent
extremes and flaunting her new acquirements before the eyes of a wondering world,

she is in part excusable ; many do the same in their efforts to appear at ease in a new position.

In time women will see how foolish they have been and how unwise is their desire to rule the universe and to oust man from his laborious position : they will then settle down quietly into their place in the world, which is certainly far from the position they have hitherto held, and it is to be hoped far from the one they apparently, at present, covet.

They need not be puppets. The Evelina style is no longer admired, but neither need they become masculine ; surely there is a happy medium between such an inanimate piece of putty and the rushing, driving female of this latter end of the nineteenth century : a woman who shall be truly womanly in her attitude toward man, the one abso-lutely necessary for the development of the other.

Woman undoubtedly resents a man's in-terference in the household ; she considers that to be her province exclusively. Then pray why not accord him the same privilege

when he takes the liberty to doubt her fit-
ness for a man's work ?

It would seem to be that what she desires is to have everything her own way and
the right to do exactly that which seems
good in her sight ; what she wants is, in fact,
precisely what she has so long and so bitterly complained of in men, the right accorded them all these ages. It looks a
little like a case of Tweedledum and Twee-
dledee.

There is much to be said on both sides.

Independence, more liberty, is their cry ;
but once they have gained that coveted
condition they are not satisfied. They demand what they call equality with men,
and, when accorded that right, complain at
the lack of courtesy shown them. Perhaps were these same women a little more
gracious in their acceptance of courtesies
they might receive them oftener. Men like
to wait upon women when they feel their
services are acceptable ; it is a pleasure to
them to feel that women are dependent
upon them. But naturally they do not like
to be ignored or treated as superfluous ;

they have held first place so long it is not
to be wondered at their objecting to step-
ping aside altogether.

It would seem to be necessary that experience remain the best teacher, and
woman will learn her lesson in that way
only, but the time will come, has come to
many, when they will realize how fortunate
they are that men are willing to care for
and protect them. True, there are many
poor women who have to make their own
way in the world, but it depends very
largely upon themselves what treatment
they receive from men. These bread-win-
ners can be an immense power for good if
they will only exert the very best that is in
them and command respect and fair treatment. A few generations of such women,
and there would be much less sin in the
world.

Nine times out of ten it is a woman's
influence makes or mars a man's life. The
women of the home begin it, the women of
the world finish it; so not until all women
are noble will all men be brave and true.

The woman who is content with a less

conspicuous sphere in life is the woman
who has time to devote herself to making
a home whose influence shall be a power
for good to all who enter its doors. Let
woman rule, if rule she must, through the
atmosphere she creates around herself;
that influence is far greater than many
of them realize. Let it be used to inspire men with noble thoughts and high
ideals.

Since Eve tempted and Adam fell woman
has been the power behind the throne ; some
of the noblest and, alas, some of the wick-
edest deeds of history have been the result
of her influence. But as two wrongs never
yet made a right, there will of necessity
have to be concessions on both sides before matters will assume a normal condition. Woman has been in bondage so
long that the fetters once loosed she will
undoubtedly often soar far beyond her
strength, and the resultant falls will cause
many bruises, but in the end they will
prove salutary, and determine conclusively
just how far she can go with safety and benefit to herself. She is at present in a tran-

sition stage, and, as every one knows, that is a most trying and ungraceful position to occupy.

Colonel Higginson puts it well when he says the wonder is not that she has done so little, but that she has done so much under the existing circumstances of the past.

All women, whether they belong to the aggressively progressive type or not, resent the false position they are at present forced to assume.

Even now a woman with brains a degree beyond the average is looked upon as somewhat of a *rara-avis*, and is accorded a half-respectful, half-grudging meed of praise ; she is considered a blue-stocking and shunned as eccentric, while a man of unusual ability is a lion among his fellows.

Well, woman will one day find her level, and when that much-to-be-desired time arrives it is to be hoped that the much-vexed question of woman and her sphere will be laid away deep down beneath the sod in a grave too deep ever to be exhumed.

FEMALES UNATTACHED AND OTHERWISE

ABSOLUTELY bewildering are the varied phases of femininity. It is not to be wondered at that woman has gained the reputation of being fickle, although in many, very many cases the accusation is a most unjust one. It is her varying moods and often apparently unaccountable actions that have gained for her this undesirable reputation.

There are as many types of womanhood as there are women in the world, for, look the universe over, no two, however much they may seem alike, but will be found to have strongly differing characteristics which give decided individuality to each.

One is obliged to keep constantly on the alert in order to meet half-way the many moods that most women will display in an hour's intercourse. And yet is it not in just that variety wherein lies the charm of the sex's personality?

Woman is bewildering, tantalizing, soothing, vexing, craving forgiveness, and meekness itself all in five minutes. No wonder men give up trying to find an explanation for it all and are forced to accept them as they are, for charming enigmas whom they could not, and would not if they could, get along without.

Still, this description does not apply to all the gender; far from it, indeed. Many would consider it a positive insult to be so classed; at least so they say, but *entre nous*, would they? The nineteenth century woman is a most complex affair; really, it is much to be doubted if one among them knows just what it is she does want. But breathe that not in Gath!

To begin with, this type of woman wants to forge ahead and keep pace with the men in all matters whatsoever, pertaining alike to things secular and religious. She wants a voice in politics, on the rostrum, in the press; in short, she wants a voice everywhere except, perhaps, in the home, and with this class of woman the home gets along quite as well without as with her, perhaps better.

Such women should belong to the band of independent females. They have no moral right to promise to make homes for men or to become mothers of children if they mean to desert such sacred duties to enter into a wider field of usefulness, as they express it. What can possibly give a wider range or grander opportunities than the position of wife and mother?

The help and comfort which only a loving wife can give to her husband, the tender sympathy which goes so far to lighten the load when he is bowed down with care and anxiety, a judicious and well-timed curtailment of expenses when money difficulties render it expedient. He is a wise man who goes to his wife when troubles environ him. Many an innocent woman has been blamed for the ruin that has come, when she has known nothing whatever of its probability. Some men are too cowardly to tell their wives of impending disaster, others, from a false sense of kindness, withhold the knowledge, and very many think them absolutely incapable of understanding anything connected with business affairs. Too often wealth, happiness, and home is sacrificed to false ideas.

When a woman becomes a mother she has assumed a position the most responsible that can come into a human life. Her opportunities are boundless, her influence without limit. It is the mothers who make the nation ; their precepts rule the world. Motherhood should be a woman's highest happiness as well as the cause of her gravest responsibility ; to assume the direction of a human life is no light task. Yet how often are these gifts of God, these sacred trusts, confided to the care of ignorant and often immoral servants, whose culpable neglect or injudicious indulgence will do more harm in a single day than years of careful training can irradicate !

"Partnership with God is motherhood ; what strength, what purity, what control, what wisdom, what love should belong to her who helps God fashion an immortal soul !"

Females Unattached and Otherwise

The unattached females, those who range from the age of twenty-five to ten years later, occupy rather a trying position ; they are no longer girls, although they feel young and most of them look so, neither are they settled-down women with an assured position of their own. They are just as capable of enjoying a good time as when they were in their teens, yet the girls of that charming age talk about them as the old girls, and consider it a bore to have them around and claiming a part in their fun. Poor things ! they do not seem to belong quite anywhere ; few find the niche they do fit into before they are forty, unless, indeed, Hymen claims them in the mean time. But by the time they reach this age most of them have settled into a groove.

Some think the hurly-burly of the outside world is where they belong, some find enjoyment and variety in club life, still others turn philanthropists. A good many, the majority it may be, find their vocations in the nurseries and by the firesides of their more attractive sisters, and there they

live out a quietly contented, colorless existence, darning the children's stockings
and looking after their welfare generally,
doing a little here, a little there, to fill in
deficiencies and make more perfect the
rounded sum of other lives.

Only too often such a complete obliter-
ation of self is accepted without a thought
or with a half-compassionate feeling of
complacency that a home is given this
sister who has no closer ties.

They do noble work in the world, these
women, and they are seldom appreciated ;
but perhaps they do not seek or require
sympathy. All honor to them ; may they
always find a warm corner in somebody's
heart and home.

There is still another class of women
who may be numbered among the unattached,—those who have cultivated their
minds a degree beyond the rest of their
kind, who have cared for the reading of
good books, or have followed out some
branch of science. The beauties of nature
and of art have meant much to them, or
they have found interest and enjoyment in

the study of their fellows. These women, whatever their station in life, have a never-failing fund of wealth to fall back upon when other sources fail. They are never lonely, seldom bored, and can always find amusement within themselves, one of the greatest blessings which can fall to the lot of a human being. A few, having exceptional talents, make for themselves name and place in the world of art or letters. But it is to be doubted if they are as happy in this glare of light as when they were resting in the kinder twilight of obscurity.

And yet, if one feels she can excel in any special direction, be it ever so little, surely it is wise and desirable to add that little to the general good. It is after the manner of thus excelling that the world has progressed. Each one adds his or her mite, and so little by little the whole has been reared.

But little by little the world is meeting with a sad and irreparable loss in a gradual dying out of its womanly women and the substitution in her place of the boisterous and aggressive female of the nineteenth century.

The past hundred years has seen no more startling or wonderful event than the change of position of its women. Is the change for the better? There used to be something almost sacred about the name of a good woman which appealed to the chivalrous in every man's nature and made the idea of protection very sweet to both. Perhaps this is too pessimistic a way of looking at the question, and as all reforms are the result of violent extremes, so probably will it be with woman and her sphere. Some day she will realize that to be born a woman is the greatest privilege bestowed upon the human race ; her opportunities are limitless, with her it rests whether that human world of which she is a part shall be ennobled or degraded, for hers is the right of motherhood, that most sacred trust which few indeed are worthy to have bestowed upon them.

CHURCH AND RELIGION

MANY and varied are the phases of religion, of that something which should be an absolute unity among all mankind; so much a thing, of course, that as a separate entity it would never be considered; as much a part of life as the air breathed; a natural atmosphere surrounding every one.

And yet there is no one thing in the history of the world which has caused more bitter quarrels, more brutal warfare.

How is it possible to suppose that a religion thrust upon a people at the point of the sword can inspire reverence and love, or can be acceptable in the sight of God !

From earliest times it has been the forms and ceremonies of the church that have caused such hot dissensions, such terrible ruptures of nations. The way in which God should be worshipped has been the all-important and much-disputed question. So important, indeed, did these matters become at one time not so very long ago, it seemed as if the first meaning was fast sinking into a secondary place, if not being overlooked altogether.

But in no one direction has the thinking man asserted himself more boldly of late years than in his attitude toward religion ; he now realizes that his professions carry far less weight than his deeds. Acts, not words, stamp the man.

But even yet the narrowness and bigotry surrounding the church is a fruitful source of evil. The day has passed for the people to accept and believe because the church says so ; there are now more thinking for themselves, believing what seems right to them, rejecting much that would have caused an earlier age to gasp with horror over the mere idea of doubting.

There are many types of Christians. The Sunday one, for example, who causes that blessed day of rest to be dreaded as one of weary misery because of his Puritanical ideas which are confined to that day alone, and, like his other Sunday garments, are laid away until another week rolls around.

Church and Religion

Another type is the indefatigable church-worker, whose time is so occupied with meetings of one kind and another that when she is at home her overwrought nerves and fatigue find vent in impatience and irritability, thus throwing another shadow over so-called religion. Such as these do infinite harm to the cause they profess to be working so earnestly to advance.

There are so many sects, so many roads, all leading to the same goal.

To the heathen (?) missionaries are sent. In one place there will perhaps be representatives of half a dozen different denominations. One point they have in common, and, as far as the church goes, one only,— they all agree upon the divinity of Jesus Christ ; but the way in which He shall be worshipped, the way in which His example is to influence their lives, is so differently put to these almost wholly ignorant, only partially civilized people, what wonder is it they find this new religion offered them too vague and unsubstantial for their acceptance ! Which one of them all is to be believed and relied upon ?

Fireside Fancies

A native of Ceylon is said to have told one of the many missionaries who visited his island that until they—the missionaries —could agree among themselves it would be worse than useless to expect others to accept their teachings.

Mohammed, to the followers of Islam, is the prophet of Allah ; to the Christian, Jesus Christ is the prophet of God. Are not God and Allah one and the same? Does not the difference in the lives of their followers come chiefly because of education? When the East accepts Western civilization the evils of their religions will right themselves.

Let those who feel their work should lie in foreign fields turn their attention to education by practical methods. Let their religion be a part of themselves, and their teaching of it be of the protecting love of God and of their duties toward their fellow-men ; that will convey far more meaning to their limited understandings than the forms and ceremonies of various sects, which only serve to confuse them.

It would simplify living very materially

if every one would do as near right as heart and conscience dictated. This world would then be a much easier place to live in. A spirit of tolerance would go a long way in the right direction.

All are striving for happiness now and hereafter; but as we live we create our own heaven or hell.

What deeds of cruelty have been done and bloody wars fought, which have brought horror, agony, and even annihilation to whole nations, all in the name of religion! Such things cannot be pleasing to a merciful Father! What difference does it make to Him whether we are called Heathen or Christian, Catholic or Quaker, so long as we live the right kind of lives? Every one knows when they do wrong, so bringing misery to themselves and sorrow to their God, sorrow because of man's weakness, not an opportunity to wreak vengeance.

The Bible and the pulpit have much to answer for in their interpretation of the God of fear.

It would be a God of cruelty who delighted thus in the torture of the creatures

He had made after His own image. If this were so, would He have made this world so beautiful and so productive, have given man a reasoning intelligence that he might use and enjoy that by which He has surrounded him? If we allow ourselves to abuse His gifts and let the Godly in our natures be gradually stamped out, surely it is our own fault! If nature's laws are transgressed, suffering is the result. It is cowardly in the extreme to attribute to Providence what is wholly the result of man's weakness.

No quarrels ever raged with more bitterness than those between church factions. The very idea conveyed by the word church should be love and unity of mankind, yet it would seem to be almost a synonyme for dissension.

Where people are met together to do church work there is much hot discussion, ending very often in open rupture, because of forms to be observed.

It is not the formal observance of religion that God cares about, but the real spirit that is shown in the daily acts of living, in man's relations and dealings with his fellow-man. That is the only religious spirit worthy the name.

Is it whether a man calls himself Christian, Buddhist, or Moslem that makes him acceptable in God's sight?

Be he Jew or Gentile, there is but one thing makes a man what his Creator intended him to be, and that is the comprehension of the fact that "the kingdom of heaven is within a man," and with himself alone does it rest whether he becomes Christ-like or tramples his God underfoot.

❧❧❧

WEIMAR AND NAISHÁPÚR

THE monotonous drip, drip of the rain outside makes even more attractive than usual the cosey library lighted only by the blazing logs ; the warm glow from which extends into the farthest corner of the room, causing many a revered object to assume an appearance positively grotesque.

The bust of the dignified Goethe might

as readily be mistaken for the likeness of a
grinning satyr as of the glorious genius of
Weimar, the author of "Faust ;" for it is to
that poem he owes his great fame, although
his genius had the rare quality of being
equally powerful in many directions.

His literary work comprises a vast series
of subjects, in each of which some special
phase of the writer's character reveals itself.
In "Faust" he is the philosopher, in "Her-
mann und Dorothea" the idyllist, in "Mar-
chen" he becomes an allegorist ; as a prose
writer alone he would have ranked among
the first of Germany's literary celebrities.
In the field of science, also, he was an acknowledged leader. Rare as such a com-
bination is, all these attributes were found in
Goethe. Added to this was the desire and
the ability to so use his talents that by his
indomitable courage and vast capacity for
making the most of these gifts he made of
himself what few men have become. An
early development of the power of self-
control was largely instrumental in bringing
about the brilliantly successful result. To
his mental acquirements health also was

added, and a life of over fourscore years
in which to accomplish the prodigious labors
of his pen. With high social position, am-
ple means, and physical beauty, surely this
man was favored by the gods.

Highly gifted, charming in manner to an
unusual degree, he attracted to his side the
intellect and refinement of the age. Men
and women alike found the charm of his
personality irresistible.

Among so many whom the Fatherland
is proud to claim Goethe stands supreme.
His influence upon his surroundings can
scarcely be over-estimated. Herder, Les-
sing, Schiller, these and many others whom
the world holds in reverence were his
friends. Their genius received impetus
from his own, to him were they indebted
for much intellectual food. But while he
gave so generously he also received incalculable benefit from intercourse with
men of such mighty powers. The world
in which he lived had as much to offer his
constructive genius as ever it could receive
in return.

Every man, great or little, has his weak-

nesses. Goethe's was a superstition regarding certain days which he considered fatal
to any undertaking begun on them, one of
these being the 22d of March, and, strangely
enough, it was on that day he died.

Pre-eminent among his works is "Faust;"
this poem, begun when he was a mere boy,
—but twenty years of age,—extended itself
over a period of sixty years, for not until
the poet was within seven months of his
death was the last line of the second part
written. Many of his contemporaries had
already produced versions of the story of
Dr. Faustus, but Goethe's is the only one
of them all which stands out fresh as the
hour when it came from the printer's hands.
Among many other works, that also was in
an unfinished state when its author took up
his abode in Weimar, where his official duties and whole mode of life so interrupted
the tenor of his thoughts and interfered
with the completion of the manuscripts
that it is probable "Faust" would have
been among those which were never finished
had it not been for the urgent solicitations
of his friends, Schiller among them ; it was

largely owing to his insistence that after a
lapse of fifteen years Goethe again took up
the thread of thought so long laid aside,
and another fragment was added. Finally,
after many delays and interruptions, the
first part was published in 1808, and a
new masterpiece took its place among the
immortal productions of man. Not until
many years had passed, and this great man
was fast nearing his end was the second
part given to the world. It has been said
that Goethe would not permit himself to die
until the whole of this work conceived in
his early youth had been finished as he intended it should be, with Faust overcoming
the wiles of Satan, with the final victory of
his hero, and his ascent into heaven. This
done, the life work of one of the world's greatest geniuses was accomplished. To the first
part of this poem is given universal acclaim.
Every one is familiar with its pages, while
many are acquainted only in a hap-hazard
way with the final scenes in this drama of a
life. Had the story of Marguerite remained
unwritten, Goethe's place in the world of letters would have ranked among the highest,

it is true, but, where now his name is known
among all classes and conditions, it would
in that case have been only the cultured
few to whom his writings appealed. He
would have been considered a man of marked
ability, perhaps might even have claimed
the title of genius, now unreservedly his.
Some one of his other works might have
given to him that rank. But it is as the
author of "Faust" that his name has become
a household word ; by that supreme pro-
duction has he become one of the immor-
tals. "Faust" was inspired ; were it not for
the fact that its author's name adorns the
title-pages of "Wilhelm Meister" and "Her-
mann und Dorothea," they would now be
little read. Fine as they are, they are yet
utterly dwarfed by the side of "Faust." Unlike as they are, comparison is impossible.
Were they each the product of a different
pen, each would stand as a type of supreme
excellence in its own special line.

The "Sorrows of Werther," vastly popular in its day, Goethe is said in later years to
have utterly condemned, and regretted ever
having written it. To the general public

his "Iphigenia at Taurus" is little more than
a name, although it has by many critics
been pronounced the finest specimen of
modern Greek tragedy, yet the ordinary
reader knows very little about it, few among
them have turned its pages. But all the
world knows of the temptations offered to
Faust by the wily Mephistopheles. Had
he never written another line, that alone
would have insured him lasting fame.

Few, indeed, are so gifted as to produce
more than one masterpiece. They may
accomplish much good work, but it is by
one supreme effort that they gain the pin-
nacle of fame. Milton's "Paradise Lost,"
Byron's "Childe Harold," Dante's "Divine
Comedy," these are incomparable and will
live forever.

To do without these classics, not only
these but many others of less pretension
yet equal worth, would rob the world of
much that it now holds dear.

Books are so much a part of life that it
is difficult to fully realize their value, or to
appreciate how much careful thought has
gone toward their making. Page after

page is skimmed over with never a moment's pause to think of what it has meant to the author ; how in his effort to make his meaning clear in the fewest words possible he has written and rewritten the sentence that now reads so easily.

There is a vast difference in the construction of sentences. Some are so involved, so hemmed around with big words, that in the effort to get at the meaning one fails to intelligently connect this latest idea with the one preceding it. Whenever a word of two syllables will adequately express a thought one of four should unhesitatingly be discarded. For why write if not to be read, and if read to be understood ?

Flaubert is said to have desired to write for a few only, but deep down in his heart must have lurked the wish to have the few expressed by an addition of numerals.

However small the circle his writings may reach, an author should not be deterred from saying what he feels may appeal to those few. To them it may be of value, and through them transmitted to others.

Weimar and Naishápúr

Probably every one has a direct mission in life if he would take the trouble to find it out; and when found, if followed up, much satisfactory work would result.

Matthew Arnold makes it very clear in these lines :

> " Bounded by themselves and unregardful
> In what state God's other works may be,
> In their own tasks all their powers pouring,
> These attain the mighty life you see."

For, after all, it is our own individual existence we have to live out, so why be continually comparing our surroundings with those of others? In the same poem he says,—

> " Resolve to be thyself, and know that he
> Who finds himself loses his misery."

Instead of following such eminently good advice and endeavoring to find our true selves, we are continually looking out for the characteristics of others bound up in our own personality, so destroying the individuality we should be forever striving to cultivate.

Originality is something rarely found, because all are trying to be like some one else. The result is a hopelessly mediocre and generally uninteresting set of people.

But when the surface self is forgotten for a time, then social intercourse becomes something more than the mere platitudes, which are all that the other phase will allow.

Where all are so impregnated with the veneer of good form, one hesitates to break through the formalities, fearing to be misunderstood ; to that fear is due much of the flippancy met with in ordinary intercourse. Each mistrusts the other.

With some poor unfortunates the lack of individuality is attributable to their half-hearted belief in the lines of old Khayyám :

> " 'Tis all a checkerboard of nights and days,
> Where destiny with men for pieces plays,
> Hither and thither moves, and mates, and slays,
> And one by one back in the closet lays."

What incentive to achievement can there possibly be with that idea for the background of life ? If there is a " destiny that shapes our ends," then we start in life pretty severely handicapped. It is much more inspiring to believe that we have something to do with the shaping of our own destinies. Omar thought much and wrote a great deal that is misleading at first sight, but one can easily read between the lines of his quatrains and gather many a meaning that the words fail to convey.

The man was centuries beyond his time. Throughout all he has written can be felt that reaching out for something just beyond his grasp; he felt there must be something tangible for which his whole soul longed, yet which he could not sufficiently fathom to quite believe in. Everything was against him, the time in which he lived, the people by whom he was surrounded. He lived in an era of materialism among a set of scoffers, so he, too, scoffed with the rest; on the surface, at least, trying as best he might to stifle his longings and ignore his uncomprehended desires; brooding in secret, expressing his ideas in grossest materialism or in tones of tenderest reverence; misunderstood by his associates, having but an uncertain knowl-

edge of himself, at one time living the life
of a Stoic, at another, if we may believe
his own words, one of wild debauchery.

Had he lived in nineteenth century civilization instead of eleventh century barbarism
his knowledge would have been more complete, his life have been one of worth and
usefulness to his world.

It is strange that this Persian poet, who
lived so long ago and who wrote so little, has
been so often translated ; that he has been
proves his genius.   Men do not waste their
time on difficult problems unless some rich
harvest is to follow.   Again and again has
he been translated, and more than once
by the same admirer ; with each new reading fresh meaning is revealed, new depths
of thought discovered : a retranslation is
the result, and again the effort is made to
express, in our practical language, the
mysticism of the original.   In a strictly
literal translation much beauty would be
lost, and would probably fail to convey to
our unoriental senses the real meaning of
the poet.

For he was essentially a poet, as is proved

by the very unsuccessful attempts to render into prose his quatrains. To convey their meaning his thoughts must needs be expressed in verse.

Rest well, Omar Khayyám ! at last the great mystery for which thou so vainly sought a clue lies unravelled before thee. Sleep well in thy quiet grave under the shadow of the roses of Naishápúr, those roses that were once so dear to thee. May their scented petals for evermore fall in silent benediction upon thy resting-place.

SOCIETY

To be in society is the much coveted goal of a multitude of people.

To be in society of the kind which is generally meant, when the word is used by the people who desire to be in it, requires but one thing. The all-powerful bank-account is the open sesame to this charmed circle. With that at his back, society opens wide its doors to the aspiring possessor, and at

once he is in the swim, rushing headlong
with the rest of the upper crust. They are
hard-working individuals, these society people. Their energy is deserving of the admiration worthy a better cause. If any one
considers the duties of a society woman
light or trivial, let them try it for a time,
and sneers will turn into awe-struck amaze-
ment that any one could be found to work
so hard for mere duty's sake, for Madame
à la Mode gets no pleasure out of this
round of gayety ; at least, so she says. She
is bored to death most of the time, and
apparently lives in daily expectation of
death from *ennui*. Surely she is a self-sac-
rificing martyr. But what is the sacrifice
for ? If for her daughters, it is certainly a
useless one, for they are bored to death
too. So if that is her only reason, it is
scarcely worth the trouble.

It is no small undertaking to meet the
demands of society, for its claims are many
and exacting. Each day brings its round
of gayety. Functions of all sorts must be
attended and suitable costumes be prepared for each. The gowns, hats, gloves,

etc., to be worn on these occasions demand more than a passing thought, and the rights of the modiste cannot be ignored if matron and maid are to appear as they should.

The giving of entertainments or paying off of social debts, as it is called, is usually a matter for grave consideration. There are half a dozen small affairs to be given to which a favored few are bidden. Then will come one grand hash party for which each one of the large circle of acquaintances receives a card. These affairs are very charming, very beautiful, as of course they should be. Being competitive shows, the last is always the most novel and the most costly. He who gives his affair early in the season is wisest. The competition is then not so great, and the strain upon his resources is not so taxing.

And so they keep it up week after week, from December until Lent comes to put a stop to the season in town. They then seek some of fashion's other resorts, only to continue the same general plan, followed by the mad rush of Easter week, after which the summer exodus begins, and more healthful amusements take the place of overheated ball-rooms. Talk about these people being idle or lazy ! They are the hardest workers of any class. They never rest until somebody dies and they are compelled for form's sake to stop a little while.

What is the charm about this kind of social life ? It does not seem to have any object, because it never advances ; it is virtually the same to-day as it has always been, —dancing, flirting, talking, and eating.

Can it be that these things so completely fill their lives and satisfy them that they never feel a desire for a more real existence ? Frosted cake is very nice, but if one never had anything else what a relief plain bread and butter would be at times !

Dancing is delightful if the floor is good and the partner agreeable. Flirting seems always to be *de riguer* in society. But as for conversation, it does not exist. Society does not converse ; it has not time. Society chats ; something quite different. And eating, though mentioned last, is by no means least, for when society entertains, more thought, care, and expense is given to eat-

ing than to all the other things put together. The feast of reason and flow of
soul style is out of date, and society, unless
it is up to date in all things, cannot hold
its own.

But there is another kind of society,
although it lays no claim to that title, where
social intercourse is held a pleasure, where
meeting and talking with one's friends is a
privilege and a relaxation from the cares of
life. Among this set what is said holds a
more important place than what is worn or
what is eaten, although they also are accorded due recognition. Nothing is more
displeasing than a carelessly dressed person, and his words, although pearls of wisdom, lose half their weight if the speaker
is unkempt and unregardful of the nice-
ties that every one is in duty bound to
observe.

Really good society is composed of people who are able to appreciate the best, and
are willing to give their best in return.

To be in this kind of society is, indeed,
something to desire and to strive for, but
the requirements for membership are be-

yond the capabilities of those who find their enjoyment in the other kind. Refinement, intellect, culture, and good breeding are the passwords that admit the bearer within these doors.

Where are the brilliant *salons* of a past century? That we do not have them now surely cannot mean that we have no minds capable of forming them! That supposition would be too humiliating. It cannot be that, for, with all the learning of the past to aid us, each succeeding generation should prove more clever than the one gone before. Everything is made so much easier for us than it was for our grandfathers. True, there is just that much more to know than there was fifty or a hundred years ago, but one need only take the best ; much of it is not worth knowing.

Perhaps one reason we do not have these brilliant gatherings is because people are too busy with their own affairs and do not feel the necessity for that pleasant mutual exchange of ideas. But it is a thousand pities that people of intellect cannot be brought more in touch with each other.

Nothing so tends to broaden the mind and enlarge the capabilities as intercourse with one's fellows. He who shuts himself entirely away from the world is doing himself a great injury. No matter how clever he may be, his horizon becomes narrowed and he himself becomes intolerant of all that does not particularly appeal to him. In a word, he loses touch with humankind, and for that reason fails to accomplish much of definite worth.

Every one can preach ; it is the easiest thing in the world to tell others what they ought to do ; but, as has been often said, "actions speak louder than words," so if we say one thing and do another, what we say carries very little weight.

CASTLES IN SPAIN

Few are so poor as to be entirely without possessions. Many, indeed most people, have extensive landed estates in Spain if nowhere else. Many of the happiest hours of life are spent within that sunny clime.

Of all kinds of real estate, it is the most comfortable to hold, for it is never in need of repairs. There are no tax-bills coming in, and no tenants demanding all sorts of et cæteras. But there it is, always as it should be, ready for occupancy at a moment's notice ; prepared alike for the coming of a large house party or for the advent of the individual owner. Spacious enough for the one, small enough for the other, a cosey retreat where loneliness is unknown, without a name.

Ah! these dream-palaces, what unbounded pleasures lie within their walls ! When once the doors close behind us absolute content reigns supreme. No one is ever unhappy there, but succumbs a willing victim to long, tranquil hours of bliss.

What lazy, delicious dreams are ours as the golden moments of idleness flit by ! In these hours the very essence of the healing balm of rest is experienced. Mind, body, and heart are absolutely at ease. But not all the hours passed in this delightful retreat are given over to idleness. Many are filled with meaning, from which spring actions strong and determined. Hours of idleness passed by the gifted ones of earth are rich in productiveness. Artists, poets, musicians, inventors, all these who make life sweet and work possible, spend their time while residents in Spain with ultimate profit to their fellow-men. Many are the divine harmonies, the exquisite lines of beauty, words that kindle the soul with noblest aspirations, and inventions that seem the work of a magician which come to us from over the border of this mystic land. They come to us because their creators have used their leisure while rambling through the flower-strewn gardens of this far-off world to piece together their thoughts and ideas, obtaining such results that miracles are constantly being enacted before our very eyes. The world could ill afford to do without its dreamers of dreams and seers of visions.

But not to all is given the ability or the methodical power necessary for the working

out of the very vague idea which, properly
handled, may result in a prime factor in the
world's history.

Other people who are not geniuses, not
even unusually clever men and women, also
inhabit their castles in Spain, and with equal
pleasure to themselves if not of equal profit
to the world.

We cannot all be geniuses, and a very
good thing it is, too. There must be some
ordinary minds to keep the balance even.
It would be too trying to one's mental equi-
librium to be forever surrounded by super-
latives ; for the master-stroke of a genius
is always a superlative in its especial field.
It takes the average individual some time
to grasp an entirely new idea, to become
accustomed to a hitherto unknown power,
to assimilate the use of the new, discarding
the old ; in a measure changing the whole
tenor of life as it becomes necessary to adopt
one's self to altered surroundings.

Just fancy having something new and
startling thrust upon our poor distracted
heads each day ! In that case we should
have to change from one thing to another

with such lightning rapidity that the result would soon be a world of lunatics.

Geniuses are glorious examples of the capabilities of man. But for the majority of humankind ordinary intelligence is better, even if they do live less exalted lives and dream far simpler dreams. Yet they, too, have Spanish estates where they spend whatever time they can afford to take from their more prosaic existence. Life there is very simple, very unworldly. No evil has as yet found admittance within the land. All is charmed peace and happiness. The sky is always blue, the air balmy, the trees, the grass and flowers never fade, but retain their greenery and fresh beauty forever. It is a land of hope and a land of promise, where all things are possible and disappointment never comes.

No one ever grows old there, no one ever dies, or, worse still, lives to embitter the lives of others, but all are true and noble.

No one enters these charmed precincts without a special invitation, so no one is ever unwelcome. There are no social debts to be paid, so hash parties are unknown. It goes without saying, therefore, that only the most delightful intercourse with kindred spirits ever takes place. How we sigh for that Acadia as we are tossed hither and yon like some helpless shuttlecock from the relentless battledoors, half crushed to death in some maelstrom of society! We are constantly being interrupted in the middle of a sentence which, it is true, had very little meaning, but it might have ended brilliantly if only we had had sufficent time to finish it. But time is something one never has in a gathering of this kind, so, after all, it really does not matter whether the sentence is ever finished or not, or, for that matter, whether it is ever begun ; some one else will say virtually the same thing. There is very little variety in society conversation, and so it is just as well to save what little breath is left to elbow one's way still farther into the crowd, and at last through it to emerge victorious from the outer door, thankful to be a free man once more.

Things are not done in that way on the

Spanish estates. Only the favored few are admitted, and there is always plenty of time to say what one wants to. And best of all, something is possible there that unfortunately is utterly impossible in any other spot on the inhabited globe, the unsaying of words once spoken ; there they can be blotted out as completely as though never uttered ; that is an inestimable boon quite worth the trouble of the trip there were it a much more difficult journey than it is, but the way is very straight, very easy to find, and very comfortable to travel over. Close the eyes, and, presto ! you are there enjoying all the delights of this enchanted land.

The return trip is just as simple, only sometimes the landing here is accompanied by rather a rude shock and the sound of a peremptory voice commanding the immediate execution of an unpleasant duty. At such times the longing for a permanent abode in that happy country is intense ; but would not even perfection pall in time ? Acadia is a thing of the past ; we are not yet ready for Utopia.

EDUCATION

FROEBEL has said, " Educate the child to look out for himself," thus suggesting education with the very beginning of life.

There is not the least doubt which makes the better man and citizen, he who relies upon himself or he who depends upon others.

If from the very beginning the little one is taught and encouraged to do for himself and what little he can for others, that idea once firmly implanted will grow with his growth, strengthen with his strength, until, when the real problems and difficulties of life present themselves, a strong, self-reliant nature is ready to meet and overcome them ; there will be no faltering, no trying to avoid the inevitable, no waiting for some one else to shoulder the responsibility. Every one has as much as he can do to manage his own affairs without assuming the burdens of some one else. In all the vital points of life one must decide for himself,

no one else can do it for him. The education of a firm will, a decided nature, and
the ability to look after one's self should
begin with the cradle days.

So many are taught to be incapable
when they are but wee toddlers. They
seem so helpless we do for them many
things they are quite able to do for themselves. Our love and tender care for
these tiny atoms of humanity very often
do them an injury, for the habit of depending upon others is not easily done
away with when once formed. It seems
to be human nature to shirk wherever it is
possible, but it goes without saying that
the principle is a bad one. Those who
stand firmly on their own feet, who meet
and overcome obstacles instead of going
around them, are much happier, for they
feel assured of their position. They have
made it for themselves and hold it by sheer
force of character. They have a right to
a voice in the affairs of the nation. They
have an identity of their own, and are not
here on sufferance, as it were.

Education is the all-important factor

in determining the position of the man.
Notoriety can be bought with money or
achieved in a variety of ways, but enduring
fame seldom comes unless through education.

Lack of knowledge will be found to lie
at the root of most evils.

It is the want of education that keeps
the masses in that position.   Ignorance is
the obstacle hardest to combat.   In this
country the people rule the nation.   We
have had abundant proofs of the disastrous
results in consequence of the ignorance
which flocks to the polling booths on
election days.   But education will develop
the masses into the individual, and as a result this unfortunate state of affairs will be
to some extent remedied.   The individual will then have a clearer idea of what
his vote means.   He will realize that
his country's prosperity means his own
prosperity.

Education opens all doors, enlarges the
capacity, receives and gives pleasure, opens
up mines of wealth where the uneducated
find only sealed volumes.

Education

Pope's statement that a little learning is a dangerous thing is very true, but follow the poet's advice and it is robbed of its dangers. All things must have a beginning, which is necessarily small. Great achievements are the results of tiny embryos of thought.

With the majority a little demands more, whether in learning, accumulation of property, or what not. Few are content to remain as they are ; aspirations of some kind animate every breast.

The trouble with so many systems of education is that they become a cramming process, with a little of this, a little of that, a few 'isms and 'ologies, and a little music, with a very limited knowledge of the arts and sciences. It amounts to very little, as a rule, because there is no real foundation to build upon. The school-days over, an education of this kind becomes a hazy memory of dog-eared text-books, distasteful tasks hurried through at a breakneck speed, and quarrels with teachers. Unfortunately, this makes the sum total of the average education of the boys and girls who throng the city schools; to this is added proficiency in dancing, good taste in dressing, and a thorough knowledge of the ways of society as under the tutelage of Mrs. Grundy. If the education is not considered complete, they go to college and accentuate the 'isms and 'ologies and make records for themselves in basket- and foot-ball. In this way are the girls and boys generally equipped for their start in life. It now depends entirely upon their personal exertions whether they make and hold worthy positions or sink into insignificance and obscurity. But this higher education, which is the name now given to a college course, is not requisite to make a clever man or woman. Some of our ablest statesmen have come from the masses, and have reached their positions through strength of character and the determination to make themselves a power in the land. They have accepted education of all kinds, whenever and wherever it was to be found. In time a few have been able to enter the ranks of polished gentlemen, but most of them remain in the rough diamond stage. They are able to accomplish a vast deal, it is true, but if to the sound judgment and good common sense were added an educated sense and a wider outlook they would become a powerful factor in the advancement of civilization ; but as they are, they are worthy of all respect and stand as an example to their kind. Every one can become an influential power if he choose, but it is to be obtained only through individual exertion.

If our public schools would turn their attention more to sensible, practical knowledge, with the idea of making labor honorable, and less to the æsthetic refinements, they would become an immense power for good and do much toward solving the socialistic problem.

Every one must work in some way save, perhaps, the tramp. Our government is so rich and generous it prefers, apparently, to support him in idleness at an enormous annual cost. But for those who do not desire to be classed along with that nomadic race of beings, work is the natural order of things, and so again education is a factor of prime importance, for it makes work easier. The know how is the straightener out of tangles. With wider knowledge comes the know how.

It is hard to make those steeped in superstitious ignorance believe this, but such a vital truth must find credence at last. All great truths force recognition.

Public libraries, art museums, and public parks are all liberal educators.

If the people are surrounded by beautiful and refining influences they unconsciously imbibe them, at first passively, then greedily, until the whole tone of their being becomes changed, more humanized.

Surroundings have a very important influence on all lives. From earliest babyhood children should live as much as possible in an atmosphere of beauty and intelligent refinement, the books and pictures given them to play with should suggest only happy thoughts, no cloud should unnecessarily darken the little horizons. Beauty and truth should become a part of their earliest memories. In this way they unconsciously acquire a love for the beautiful and a knowledge of the best. Good taste once gained rarely becomes vitiated.

Education is the key-note to existence, it is the civilizer of the world. All great reforms have come because of education. With increased desire on the part of the people for more knowledge higher aspirations will be born, better surroundings will follow, and the world will become more enlightened and easier to live in.

MUSIC

WITH the creation of birds music came into the world, of their vocal utterances was born a boon to mankind. With the creation of man came appreciation and enjoyment of sound and the desire to imitate. What delight and surprise must have resulted from the first human attempt to reproduce the tones of his feathered neighbor, —what unqualified satisfaction to find that he too could emit harmonious sounds!

Fireside Fancies

With the birth of music a humanizing element was introduced into the world which has proved its efficacy by the hold it has upon all people. No nation is so barbarous but it has something analogous to the music of civilization, something which charms and soothes the savage breast, although it is as unlike the harmonies to which a more æsthetic people is accustomed as two things bearing the same name well could be. Crude as it is, it meets their needs far better than would the divine strains of Beethoven or Mozart. The music of the Chinese to the ears of an Oriental is exquisite and uplifting, while to the uneducated Western taste it is quite without meaning; more than that, for its thin, shrill notes, amusing at first because of their oddity, become positively disagreeable to one accustomed to the full, rich tones of an organ swelling out in the grand chords of the Messiah.

All nations from their very inception have had music in some form as a part of the national life.

Among people of education it is refining

and humanizing to a degree ; it appeals to all the finer sensibilities ; through it the soul's altitude is expressed as it can be in no other way ; longings, aspirations, hopes, all find voice through the medium of musical sounds.

From the first gay-plumaged songster, whose privilege it was to bring so great a gift to earth, has been evolved the music which stirs the hearts of all people to-day. Very gradual has been the transition from the first crude efforts of primitive man to this epoch where the voice of God may be heard in the rolling tones of the organ.

Of all the arts, music appeals most to the senses ; it has become so much a part of life as to amount almost to a necessity. Among the æsthetics it ranks first, but what a different meaning the word conveys to each individual mind ! Sitting with closed eyes listening to the grand, inspiring chords of the masters, every fibre of one's being seem to vibrate in response. All the realities of life with its petty cares and worries seem left far behind in a dim, shadowy past. The present is the real. The soul is thrilled with pure and noble thoughts ; to live in unison with the present mood seems easy ; there must be something more in life than the struggle for existence and the everlasting scramble after the almighty dollar. After such an experience it is almost with a shock one returns to earth, to the consciousness of every-day life and to the realization that the world of harmony has not yet become a practical place to live in.

Beethoven's sonorous harmonies, Handel giving fitting utterance to religious themes, Mozart's tuneful, tender tones, these and many others have left an ineffaceable impression upon the world. Not only the masters of composition, but the lesser lights as well, have left their mark. To meet the needs of the people music must be as varied as humanity itself ; it is a civilizer of barbarous people and a humanizer of civilized people.

It is a tremendous step from Wagner to the latest popular song shouted in stentorian tones by every little street Arab. Yet so nicely is the chasm bridged across that not even a crack may be found between.

The gradation is gradual but complete; each step of the way appeals to some one capacity. Each one selects from the riches before him that which meets his need; there is no lack of variety from which to choose either in style or in the medium used. The enjoyment derived from the strains of a fine symphony orchestra is thoroughly satisfying. There is about it no disintegrating of parts, it is as one perfect whole, not a sound of many instruments but of one, magnificently sonorous, perfect in modulation, complete in harmonies, floating out and fading away into melodious space.

Probably there is no other one thing that has given more universal pleasure than music in its varied phases : even hopeless mediocrity is not only accepted, but in many cases is actually enjoyed. In these days almost every house holds a piano, and as a matter of course the occupants of that house use and enjoy it; even if the music is not of a very high order or the musician a skilled one, it yet gives pleasure to those who love the performer. When

weary in mind and body it is soothing and
restful in the extreme to sink into a cosey
arm-chair and listen to the voice of one
dear filling the soft firelit twilight with low,
sweet sounds ; tender, almost melancholy,
do they seem until with the coming of the
lights the music assumes a livelier tone, and
that delightful, mystic hour is gathered in
by relentless time to join those other dead
and gone hours of happiness.

Who that has once been so fortunate as
to hear a really fine violinist can ever forget the almost supernatural tones brought
by his skill from the senseless instrument
of wood and strings ! In the hands of the
artist it has become a living thing ; no other
instrument is so human in its tones, so
capable of expressing the individuality of
the performer, the passions of a human
soul. Plaintive and wild, it seems trembling and sobbing in an agony of grief,
wailing like a lost spirit condemned to
eternal punishment, or again it is all sup-
pressed excitement, with wild bursts of de-
lirious laughter, or the mood is dreamy
and soft, when one scarce dares to breathe

lest he lose the faint vibrations, the distant echoes of the now silent melody. But most divine of all is the music of a human voice emanating from a soul within. In its highest sense music is divine, for among all people and in all ages it has been used in connection with religious rites. Chris tian and Pagan alike have found in it fit ting expression for the worship of their deities.

Even the much maligned hand-organ is not altogether an evil, for it brings joy to the hearts of the street urchins. Its horribly garbled renderings are quite satisfying to them, and the antics of the miserable little monkey amuse and keep them out of mischief; for a time the sights and sounds of city life have lost their attraction.

"Music is a moral law. It gives a soul to the universe, wings to the mind, flight to the imagination, a charm to sadness, gayety and life to everything. It is the essence of order, and leads to all that is good, just, and beautiful, of which it is the invisible, but nevertheless dazzling, passionate, and eternal form."

SPRING

I

THE majority of women must have each season what they call a new spring suit. To Mother Nature must the same privilege be accorded ; and right gayly does she use the right to assume each year a beautiful new garb. Rather juvenile, do you say, for so old a woman ? Ah ! but remember, women are never any older than they look, and surely none look more youthful and beautiful than this generous, bountiful mother ! Each spring she awakens from her long winter's nap more fresh and radiant than ever. She looks a little tired and faded as the long nights come on and the chills of autumn fill the air. But then who would not be weary after so many months of ceaseless toil? She is glad when her work is finished and she can go to rest and seek that best restorer, sleep. For her, at least, it is a panacea for all ills. In the early spring, before the snow has quite disappeared from the hill-tops, she is aroused by the sweet note of the bluebird, that hardy little fellow who first ventures back to the bleak and arid fields, assuring us by his cheerful song that spring will not now be long delayed. With renewed vitality she awakes and hastens to drain the cup of her annual draught from the fountain of youth. She is ready then to don her gayest apparel. She seems, indeed, a very child, so riotously does she indulge her fancy for gay trimmings on her many-shaded green gowns. For, after all, green is her favorite color. Just at first she is a little timid in the matter of decorations, and for a time uses only white and violet, but soon getting bolder, she introduces a touch of yellow here and there, quickly followed by gayer reds and pinks, until she is fairly a blaze of glory. Surely no other woman could combine so many colors with so harmonious an effect!

Although so bright and joyous, usually she has her times of displeasure, when frowns gather upon her brow. But not less beautiful is she to look upon in her passion than in her hours of calm serenity. Truly sublime is she in the awfulness of her wrath, when the echo of her voice is heard in the rolling thunder and a swift glance catches the lightning-flash of her eye. But she is slow to wrath, and after such an ebullition of temper seems craving forgiveness for having caused so much disturbance, and tries to atone for her fault by making herself more beautiful than before, becoming radiant with countless flashing jewels sparkling in the sunlight, while above her head hangs a rainbow halo of glory. She humbles herself in her desire to propitiate her children, yet at the same time she is demanding their homage, a tribute always willingly paid to beauty.

But even to her come long days of darkness, when she weeps and weeps, refusing to be comforted, until from very weariness her tears are spent. Then the sun, which through all her time of grief has hidden his face in despair, shines forth and dries her eyes with his caresses, and once more she smiles upon the world, making glad the heart of man. For this same man can never accustom himself to the many phases of woman's nature. He is very dependent upon her for his comfort. Her smiles or frowns have much to do with the making or the marring of his happiness. In common with the rest of her sex, Mother Nature must consent to bear the imputation of being considered fickle. But it is a fault easily forgiven one who is so true and generous in such a multitude of ways.

II

Spring,—the most wonderful of resurrections! Look where you will a new life is seen springing from what is apparently dead. Tender blades of grass push up through the hard brown earth. Delicate new leaves, the tenderest touch would bruise or break, force their way out from the solid branches of the trees, yet these tiny shoots of green come forth fresh and perfect and expand into full growth and beauty.

Fireside Fancies

From absolute seeming deadness all nature is quivering with vitality.

But even more wonderful is the new life of the insect world. It seems incredible that anything so airily beautiful as the dragonfly can come from the sluggish grub living out its allotted time on the muddy bottom of some wayside pond. Finally, feeling a necessity for something different, it crawls laboriously up the stem of some tall water reed and there waits until its bonds are loosed, when from this almost helpless thing bursts forth an exquisite creation. One moment this green-and-gold beauty pauses uncertain, trying to realize the marvellous change that has overtaken him, then skims lightly away over the surface of his old home. Hither and thither he darts in a perfect ecstasy of delight, fairly intoxicated with this strange new freedom.

When the cicada outgrows his shell and leaves it clinging to the rough bark of a tree or on a bush, does he ever give a thought to what he so lately was as he flits through the air on his gauzy iridescent wings? When the resurrection came for

Spring

him he had ceased to need his old body ; it had served its purpose, but its day was past. Who can say if he even knew when the change took place ? It must surely be a change for the better, for in this new existence he seems as free as air.

Some such miracle is constantly taking place. One must, indeed, be wilfully blind who will deny the existence of what his own eyes assure him is being enacted before him ; for himself he can see the resurrection of an ego into a new environment.

Perhaps God has made it possible for man to witness this change in a lower form of life that he may feel assured that a freer existence awaits him also. He does not demand a blind trust from any one, but only asks that we come to Him with a confidence born of intelligence. The greater our knowledge the more reverently do we bow before the God whose simplest works are so wonderful. 'Tis only the grossest, most inexcusable fanaticism will deny the existence of a Being whose power is infinite. Every tiny blade of grass is witness to it. Every breath we draw, every movement is

made possible by some unexplainable, con-
trolling force. Call it what you will, whether
you give it the name of God or some other
title, it means the same thing, it is the same
marvellous influence that causes this immense globe we inhabit to turn on its axis
in its own infinitesimal portion of space,
that each year causes the blossoms to
mature from tiny bits of beauty into life-
sustaining elements for man. Without
God's help it would be impossible for man,
with all his intelligence and ingenuity, to
make even so much as one blade of grass
or one small leaf appear.

And yet there are men who will scoff at
the idea of a Supreme Being ! Pity them,
for they are beneath contempt in their
dense ignorance. They refuse to see that
the heavens declare the glory of God, or
that the firmament showeth His handi-
work.

III

Another pleasure the spring brings with
it is the enjoyment of watching the ever-
changing woods and fields. From the time
the first faint green is visible until at last

the whole earth glows with the luxuriant beauty of early summer. Every leaf, every blade of grass seems animated with life, bursting with joy at freedom from the long winter's bondage. So wonderful, so incomprehensible, are these changes that it seems almost a desecration to speak of them. The uncertain lights and shadows and vague, hazy distances softening all into one vast impressionist picture.

The presumption that can put upon canvas great dabs of purple, yellow, and green, labelling them impressionist views of country scenes, is something quite beyond the comprehension of a real lover of nature. Surely the painters of such pictures must use their imaginations in place of their eyes! Nature's hazy outlines and uncertain vistas cannot be reproduced.

To live near to nature makes one tender and susceptible to all that is true and beautiful. Country sights and sounds for those who have eyes and ears for them are far more refining than any to be found within the confines of city life. The country makes of a man a dreamy *dilettante*. He who cannot afford the luxury of so living had best keep away from the seductive beauties of nature.

WEALTH

WEALTH is a power, whether for good or evil lies with the possessor. Rightly used, it is the instrument of incalculable good ; wrongly used, it is a curse to the individual owner and to all who come under his influence.

Much complaint is made in regard to the unfair division of riches. But is the division so unfair ? As a rule, the man who is possessed of large wealth has worked hard, economized carefully, and been mindful of little things ; he has demonstrated his right to become a rich man by the way in which he has used brain and hands, and has proved the old maxim, The world owes every man a living, to be true. It is true, and will be given to every one who has energy and common sense.

Wealth

Given equal advantages, two men will start in life side by side. In ten years one will be in comfortable circumstances, the other in debt and barely able to keep his head above water. Why? Because one has utilized all his opportunities, has never used two dollars when one would do ; the other has considered it mean and niggardly to look after the pennies, and with lordly improvidence has squandered dollar after dollar on nothing ; when he should have been accumulating a competence he has been recklessly wasting the little he already had along with the best years of his life. Want and wretchedness are his daily companions, and his one topic of conversation is a railing at fate as to the unfair division of wealth.

He who works hard for his money knows how to appreciate it and use it carefully. The inherited fortunes are the only ones that are likely to prove a curse.

Many fortunes are made and lost in an hour, but such wealth will generally be found resting upon very unstable foundations ; very frequently depending upon the fluctuations of the stock market. No wonder a man becomes old before his time and a nervous wreck when he spends his days watching the ticker. When stocks go up he has made a good deal, and in a fever of excitement rushes off buoyed up with the hope of effecting another ; quite ignoring the fact that his success in the mad game generally means the ruin of some one else and often disgrace as well. It is a wild delirium these men live in. What wonder their lives so often end in tragedies !

Fortunes are made much slower when legitimate means are used, but is money the only good ? Is not a mind at ease with money matters in a normal condition worth untold millions that are so uncertain ? Money made and saved by judicious economy is much more likely to last. When it comes rapidly it generally goes in the same way.

Where an income is more than sufficient for the daily needs, and after the yearly nest-egg has been added to the little store, it is wise to spend the remainder. A miser is as bad as a spendthrift, and the hoarding of money helps to bring about panics in the mercantile world.

They say money is harder to make and harder to keep than it used to be, but if it were would it be spent so freely? Everything is becoming more and more beautiful, and such things as are really good are very costly. So much more is necessary now than used to be required ; the luxuries of fifty years ago are to-day numbered among the necessities.

But then, again, money goes farther than it used to, for many things are much cheaper ; those articles which are growing more costly are only bought by an occasional Crœsus, or by those who value their possessions in accordance with their cost. With taste a little will go a long way in beautifying the surroundings, and while the aforetime luxuries have become necessities, they are no longer the occasion of great expense, and many of the necessities of earlier days have been done away with entirely. The world has in a measure been reconstructed in the last fifty years.

Fireside Fancies

Yet is the way of living now more excessive than in times gone by? Court circles and the upper strata of society of all ages, going back to the earliest days of which history gives any record, have been steeped in extravagance. Barbaric splendor has not been confined to the nations of the East, but has entered largely into the surroundings of all civilized countries.

Plate and jewels, velvets and brocade, palaces with lackeys at every turn, all these were considered necessary at one time in order that the man of wealth should live up to his position. Now there is a more independent spirit displayed. The rich man can live as pleases him best. If it is his pleasure to live in a palace, they are to be had on every hand, and he assumes of his own free will the accompanying cares and responsibilities, which are by no means trivial.

It is a serious matter to be the owner of great wealth. So much is expected; however much may be done, more is demanded. Every dollar given is expected to be multiplied by ten. A man who is thought to have large means is the butt of every beggar who ever heard of him. It is five dollars here, ten there, a hundred some other place, or a few thousands as an endowment fund. Each has his own pet scheme for which he asks and expects to receive, thinking that for so worthy a cause a little at least might be given. These good people seem quite to forget that their particular hobbies have not the slightest interest for their victim, who, as a rule, knows nothing whatever about them, or, knowing, may disapprove, whereas he has of his own and those of which he does approve and wants to help, more, much more, than he is able to do. Generally, and here in America especially, he has made his own money by honest labor. Why, then, should he not spend it as seems best in his judgment?

Rich people as a class are looked upon with envy. They are supposed to have everything they want and plenty of leisure to do as they please. As a matter of fact, they are very busy people, for the many cares attending the management of a large estate require the owner to be constantly on the alert if things are to go right. There are a thousand and one things to be looked after that the poor man or he in moderate circumstances knows absolutely nothing about. The conscientious rich man is not to be envied.

Least of all are the butterflies of life to be envied,—those who float in the sun's rays until clouds obscure them. If for a moment the serious side does present itself, they push it aside, they will have none of it. Flitting from pleasure to pleasure, they live on excitement, their whole existence is passed in a feverish, unhealthy atmosphere, with inevitable collapses at the end. Even while it lasts, enjoyment of life by such cannot continue, nothing interests them for any length of time, and living becomes one long season of *ennui*. Surely one must pity the victim rather than envy a state that causes such a condition!

The people who are reckoned just comfortable are after all the ones who are best off. Nothing unusual is expected of them. They live along quietly and unobtrusively, giving what they can, taking such pleasures as they are able to afford with a feeling of well-earned reward. No one criticises the wisdom of what they do so long as they pay their bills. No one is continually spoiling their pleasure in an innocent indulgence by hinting to them that the money might better have been spent elsewhere. Those who jog along quietly in the twilight of obscurity are by far the happiest. Living on stilts is extremely wearisome.

HOURS LOST AND HOURS GAINED

"Lost,—one golden hour set with sixty diamond minutes; finder will be suitably rewarded." So the notice read, but it is not recorded that the reward was ever applied for.

The hours pass silently, relentlessly, over the heads of those who value them with the same unswerving, quiet haste as over those who value them not; who appear to think that those same golden hours can at any time be reclaimed and the opportunities that came with them be called back and taken advantage of.

But they are gone, irretrievably gone, numbered with the things of the past, and with them has gone something of life itself, the mental as well as the physical, for unless the passing hours are taken advantage of to stimulate and strengthen the growth of the mental powers, they become less and less capable of effort with advancing time, and in consequence man sinks lower, nearer the animal level, where instinct with a limited amount of intelligence prevails. But so limited are these faculties that since man came to inhabit the earth he has, because of his superior mentality, held easy supremacy over all other animals. With the slowly rolling centuries he has become the creature of to-day, as unlike those first tribes of wild human bipeds as the megatherium of prehistoric times is unlike the trained domestic animal of this era.

Had man not been endowed with intellect his place in the world would have been a far different one, and that world itself would have been something so unlike that which science, the result of intellect, has made it, that it is impossible to even fancy what it might have been had man been given instincts only.

Yet, with all these ten or twelve thousand years of which there are fairly authentic records, and of the thousands which must have preceded them, when man thought only of his daily needs, and any idea of leaving data for posterity was alike unknown and uncared for by him, has the world become so very civilized, has man taken advantage of the time given him to make of himself what he might have become?

Hundreds and thousands of years have passed, yet there seems to be no other way of settling disputes between nations now than there was in the beginning. Lives, property, often national honor, are sacrificed in testing the strength of the still semi-barbarous people who look upon war in any other light than that of the most wholesale, horrible massacre of human beings. To-day, as at all times, that nation is strongest that can hold out longest. The question is decided not by her commerce, not by her scientific gifts to mankind, not by her moral worth and her men of brains, but by the amount of powder, shot, and provisions she can supply to her armies. While this state of affairs exists is the meaning of civilization understood?

When men look lightly upon murder, stealing, and licentiousness, how many of those precious golden hours set with the diamond minutes must have been wasted!

Idle hours are not necessarily wasted hours. Some of the richest fancies, many of the most useful inventions, are evolved from these apparently unoccupied minutes, the results of which lighten the loads of millions of people. The fancies, by giving rest, recreation, pleasure, and food for thought; the inventions, by actually assisting in the routine work of the multitude, who earn their bread by the sweat of the brow rather than by the no less arduous if rather more inspiring work of the brain. Such hours, then, cannot be called wasted, no matter how idle the individual may seem mingling in some gay scene which to a casual observer may appear the very essence of thoughtless existence.

If poets and authors held aloof from all such gatherings and sat patiently at desk, pen in hand, awaiting the divine flash of inspiration that was to make them famous, very doubtful is it whether that inspiration would ever have come without the experience so necessary to aid and enrich the imagination. Even where so-called fiction is concerned, some slight foundation is necessary for the most towering flights of fancy.

For material of a sterner mould the inventor also must mix with the people, otherwise he knows not their needs, and the impetus to his imagination, for such it necessarily is in the beginning, is wanting.

For thought which assists progress of any kind, hours, even years, must be given to apparent idleness. Claude Tillier said the time which is best employed is that which is lost. That sounds like rather a broad assertion, yet there is a vast deal more in it than a first thought would suggest.

The manual laborer as well as the intellectual worker must lose many hours that he may gain others. Health and strength are his prime requisites, therefore recreation and rest are his daily needs. Nature's demands must be obeyed. In his case, also, time lost is, without doubt, time gained.

A careful apportionment of the hours does much to economize time. A methodical doing at the right time of what must be done saves many a minute in which much may be accomplished. Change of occupation is always restful. Fresh material, new interests, are continual requirements if really good results are to be obtained in anything.

It is generally those who accomplish the least who never have time for anything. The busy people, the world's real workers, have not time not to take time. Their days and years are filled with a fulness of interest of which the busy idlers do not even dream. They know that if any good work is to result time must be taken, the hours must be given to bring it to perfect fruition.

There have been occasional spurts of genius from the idlest, most useless of men. One admires but at the same time pities most profoundly the person who can so waste his talents, and who so defrauds himself and others. What he says or writes is really worse than useless, because his own life either utterly contradicts his precepts or is the saddest example of his warnings.

The time given to each individual is, indeed, short. But with each succeeding generation the opportunities are greater. To-day men can start from a basis of actual facts which even fourscore years ago it was as impossible to know anything about as it is at present to write a trustworthy treatise on the state of society and civilization in the year of grace nineteen hundred and ninety-eight.

With such a treasury of knowledge ever open to call upon in whatever direction is prompted by the inclination ; with the labor-saving, therefore time-gaining, inventions of the age, who has the right to shield

himself under the excuse that time has
been denied him in which to accomplish
some little work,—to give some slight press-
ure to the lever that is gradually raising the
world to a better and clearer understanding
of what life should mean?

CULTURE

For the intellectual health of the family
it is almost a necessity to have easy and
frequent access to a well-filled library. The
books found in a house are generally in-
dicative of the thought and character of its
inmates. A well-thumbed volume is an
intellectual photograph of the owner. But
go farther than the title, read the pages,
especially those lines which are marked ;
read also the notes scribbled here and there
along the margins, and after a careful study
of two or three such volumes belonging to
the same person it will not be difficult to
form a fairly just estimate of his character.

Something more to be desired than gold

are the well-filled book-shelves of the stu-
dent, where the genius of the world is gathered together awaiting but the outstretched
hand of the owner to give to him whatever
he is intellectually capable of grasping. The
wisdom of all ages stands waiting at the
door of his mind to confirm, suggest, or re-
fute his own preconceived notions. His
theories are to a great extent strengthened
or discarded in comformity to the books he
reads and makes a part of his life. Better
to read one good book, know it thoroughly,
make it in very truth a part of life, rather
than skim through a hundred to retain but
a vague idea of their contents when the
last volume is closed. That is not reading,
except the merely mechanical part of it, a
reading with the eyes but not with the mind ;
a pure waste of time ; better a thousand
times be idling in the fresh air of the out-
door world, so gaining bodily vigor, for the
other only tends to weaken both mind and
body. But to read understandingly, gaining the full meaning of each well-rounded
sentence, adds a richness to life than which
nothing is more compensating. For if the

mind be well-stored, it will be impossible to
be wholly miserable for long even in the
darkest hours.   Other pleasures pall in time,
but with each fresh feast the lover of books
is more eager for the next.

To read well is not necessarily to be cultured ; that is something more than mere
book knowledge, although it is a very
essential part of it.   To be a person of
culture one must know many things and
know them well.   A smattering of this,
that, and the other may show to advantage
and deceive for a time, but to the observant
it is soon evident that it is a surface knowledge only, not to be depended upon.   To
be really cultured requires strenuous effort,
and the price to be paid for it is eternal
vigilance.   For one thing, it means to know
and to be able to appreciate the best
in many directions ; literature, art, music,
science, each is an inexhaustible treasure-
house open to the man of culture.   He must
know much and think comprehensively on
many subjects.   It is not enough that he
read an article on some question of importance from an accredited source, and for that

subject adopt the author's views as his own ; but he must read many authors, think much for himself, and, if possible, obtain some practical experience, then thoroughly sift and digest, for then and then only is he competent to have an opinion that will carry weight.

Intellectuality, culture, and refinement, —the three are often confounded, but while culture is rarely, perhaps never, found unaccompanied by the other two, it is quite possible to be either intellectual or refined and yet not be both. Refinement is innate ; culture and intellect are acquired. An intellectual person may be an absolute boor, utterly indifferent, perhaps even antagonistic, toward the comforts and æsthetics of life. True refinement may be quite ignorant of all the 'isms and 'ologies, may not know a Raphael from a pre-Raphaelite, Milton may be but a name only, merely an empty sound ; yet such are often of the salt of the earth.

The seeking after culture is not without danger. As the horizon broadens and the mind becomes more and more receptive,

better able to understand and value that
which lies before and on all sides waiting to
be explored, it unconsciously assumes an
attitude of superiority over others whose
tastes or whose capabilites do not tend in
the same direction. Yet these people, if less
cultivated, are of equal value, filling their
niche in the world, doing their duty according to the light which is theirs, but in comparison they are as a tallow dip to the
electric rays radiating from culture. The
danger then lies in ignoring,—treating con-
temptuously those whose minds are not attuned to the egotists, for that he will find it
all too easy to become ; the difficulty will
be in avoiding it ; and while the term cultured cannot be denied him, yet if with all
his appreciation and interest in what is
good and great the one essential touch,
toleration, is still wanting, he has failed to
lay the most important stone in the whole
foundation.

Rather than assume the *rôle* of egoist
because of the little knowledge acquired,
it would seem that from that coign of van-
tage he was better able to appreciate his

ignorance of much to which he could never hope to attain in one short life, to say with Socrates, "I am indeed the wisest man, for I know that I know nothing."

Know thyself, said Thales ; good advice, indeed. But how many follow it? It would be a very firm foundation on which to build a life. Little danger in that case of carping at the frailties of others.

If to become cultured is to think lightly or condemn all persons and things not excelling in excellence, is it not something to be avoided rather than sought for? But why confine culture to the mind, why not cultivate the moral qualities and tender heart sympathies? Why think of culture as something connected with the intellect only? In that case it becomes mere pedantry, and drifts in one of two directions,—dilettanteism or a desire to raise the masses. Realizing from personal experience the inestimable benefits to be derived from wider knowledge, in a spirit of kindness they wish to help others attain to a like plane. But, as a rule, such people are unfortunate in the way they go about what they call raising the masses. In the very beginning they overpower them with a display of knowledge, utterly crush them under the sense of their own ignorance. While one in twenty may have the courage and the ability to rise above this and to appreciate what a real if mistaken kindness has to offer, the other nineteen are completely confused under a shower of words which, to their limited understanding, convey nothing but a series of sounds ; so culture is not just the right word to apply in such a case ; the real actuating principle is something other than that. The real thing is something that the possessor, knowing its worth, desires to share with all. Matthew Arnold describes this most aptly : of real culture he says, "It does not try to teach down to the level of inferior classes ; it does not try to win them for this or that sect of its own with ready-made judgments and watchwords. It seeks to do away with classes ; to make the best that has been thought and known in the world current everywhere ; to make all men live in an atmosphere of sweetness and light, where they may use ideas as it uses them itself, freely, nourished and not bound by them." This is the result of real culture; it seeks to humanize knowledge; to make known in all circles the best and only the best. But until the best only is current coin among people of education and social position, how is it possible for those who occupy a different level, and who look to their so-called superiors for example, to be very different from what they now are? Ignorance and vulgarity are even less attractive tricked out in broadcloth and sables than under home-spun and calico. When such people are not only tolerated, but are even courted among those who ought to demand cour-tesy and good breeding, merely because they have either a birthright membership or have bought their way into good so-ciety, what wonder that unlettered igno-rance scoffs at the true as well as the false, and that anarchy and socialism are rife, and will continue so until the masses cease through education to be the masses and become individuals. But to become educated is a slow process, and requires more than a knowledge of the little boy's three R's. To become cultured is another thing, and is purely a matter of choice, but it is not at all necessary in order to raise the public welfare from a social and political stand-point.

THE END